also by quentin tarantino

PULP FICTION
(Miramax Books/Hyperion, 1994)

FOUR ROOMS
(Miramax Books/Hyperion, 1995)

new york

from dusk

screenplay by quentin
tarantino

story by robert
kurtzman

film directed by robert
rodriguez

till dawn

Tarantino, Quentin.
    From dusk till dawn / screenplay by Quentin Tarantino ; story by Robert Kurtzman ; film directed by Robert Rodriguez.—1st ed.
        p.   cm.
    ISBN 07868-8175-5
    I. Kurtzman, Robert.   II. From dusk till dawn (Motion picture)
III. Title.
PN1997.F7466T37   1995
791.43'72—dc20   95-44650
                                                        CIP

Designed by Kathy Kikkert

FIRST EDITION

10 9 8 7 6 5 4 3 2 1

Dedicated to
Scott Spiegel,
who gave me the greatest gift,
a career

FOREWORD

A true vampire is, at its cold heart, indiscriminate. It goes where its needs take it, the necks of the high-born and the low deemed equally valuable. As long as there's a pulse, they're to the purpose. Little wonder then that the vampire has experienced a return to favour: It shares with our culture the instinct of the scavenger. Impurity is the mode of the moment; we seek out and celebrate art that revels in its own promiscuity, taking vigour from whatever veins the artist lays his or her hungry eye upon.

All of which makes Quentin Tarantino fit for induction into the league of the living dead at his earliest convenience, for there's surely nobody working in the heat of the popular gaze who has so successfully shed, mingled, and prospered upon blood from such a variety of sources. In his neo-noirs, *Reservoir Dogs*, *True Romance*, and *Pulp Fiction*, low comedy, high melodrama, hip tunes, and mesmeric violence are fused by the sheer force of his storytelling, his characters as addicted to the ephemeral pleasures of a hamburger or their own chatter as their creator. It's an infectious delight. Once bitten, we're laughing along with Quentin's happy monsters as they taunt, torment, and slaughter one another.

From Dusk Till Dawn opens in this same terrain: a place where violence is arbitrary and cruelty more likely to evoke guilty laughter than censure. But the road trip Quentin's characters (good, bad, confused, and simply crazy) undertake soon leads them astray, and halfway through the movie Quentin the screenwriter, Quentin the actor, and director Robert Rodriguez get to play a very different set of variations. The thriller grows fangs, the bullets are passed over in favour of holy water, and we're in the midst of a high-octane vampire flick.

This is not, need I say, the *fin de siècle* world conjured by a sensualist like Anne Rice, in which the melancholy undead brood and swoon in one another's arms. Tarantino and Rodriguez have created a nest of banshee vampires stripped of poetry or doubt. Nor do they seem to be an endangered species. They swarm over the screen in screeching waves of virulent appetite, their horde thinned only at terrible cost to our dubious heroes.

Rodriguez stages these action scenes in hip, comedic style, the moodier, more realistic tone of the first half of the picture abandoned as the body count grows and the rules of combat become more rococo. If we were disturbed by some of the earlier passages, it was because they had some connection to the context of the Six O'Clock News, but once the dance of the vampires begins the carnage becomes so excessive that the grimmest moments seem playful, driven by a mixture of gags and gore that recalls Sam Raimi's *Evil Dead* series.

That's not the only point of reference, of course. This is a vampire flick made by men who know the horror tradition. Peter Cushing, Hammer's great star and (for me, at least) the definitive Van Helsing, gets a nod, so—in the sheer relentlessness of the enemy—do Romero's zombie films, along with pictures by Carpenter and Polanski. There are a host of incidental pleasures besides the grue: a parade of skin-flick sex goddesses, a list speech as sleazy as it is exhaustive, a plethora of state-of-the-screen transformations and resurrections. There's also a complete disregard for the conventional niceties of who survives and who goes down spurting. In truth, it's hard to know which side truly wins the night, but who's counting?

All of this is too much chaotic fun to be frightening, of course. The film doesn't have the patience for anxiety or dread: It wants blood. The spirit of Dracula—urbane, discreet and chilly—has no place at the party Tarantino and Rodriguez are throwing. It's an all-nighter for the vampire babes and their bat-brute lovers; Dracula's Old World manners would be absurdly out of place.

He might be more than a little envious too, seeing Tarantino unapologetically supping from whatever vein suits him. It's a lesson in the modern method, and while the age applauds Quentin, Dracula will have to sulk in his grave awhile. The title of Vampire King is somebody else's for the night.

CLIVE BARKER
Kauai
Hallowe'en 1995

FADE IN:

1 EXT. LIQUOR STORE—DAY

A convenience store in a Texas suburb. No other businesses surround it.

CLOSE-UP: A light switch is flipped on.

The sign on top of the store lights up. It reads: "BENNY'S WORLD OF LIQUOR."

SUBTITLE APPEARS AT BOTTOM OF SCREEN:

BIG SPRING, TEXAS
109 MILES WEST OF ABILENE
345 MILES EAST OF THE MEXICAN BORDER

A Texas Ranger patrol car pulls into the parking lot and a real live Texas Ranger, EARL McGRAW, steps out. McGraw is in full Ranger uniform—button shirt, cowboy hat, boots, mirrored shades, tin star, and a Colt revolver on his hip.

It's about an hour and a half before sundown and McGraw is off duty for the day.

The only other car in the parking lot is a 1975 Plymouth.

2 INT. BENNY'S WORLD OF LIQUOR—DAY

A young Hawaiian shirt-wearing man named PETE sits on a stool behind the counter.

A few CUSTOMERS fiddle about.

A MAN wearing a black suit, and wire-rim glasses holds hands with a PRETTY BLOND GIRL in cutoffs and bare feet. They look through magazines.

Another black suit–wearing MAN holds hands with a RED-HEADED GIRL in a prep school uniform. They look through the beer cooler in the back of the store. Both girls are around seventeen.

McGRAW enters the store.

> McGRAW
>
> Hot goddamn day!

> PETE
>
> Haven't felt it a bit. Been inside with the air conditioner blastin' all day long.

> McGRAW
>
> Not even for lunch?

> PETE
>
> I'm by myself today, ate my lunch outta the microwave.

McGraw walks over to the beer cooler, as if done ritually every night (it is), takes out a beer, pops it open, and joins Pete by the front counter.

> McGRAW
>
> Jesus Christ, man, that microwave food'll kill ya as quick as a bullet. Those burritos are only fit for hippies high on weed. Pull me down a bottle of Jack. I'm gettin' tanked tonight.

PETE

Whatsamatter?

McGRAW

(sighs)

Awww, it's just been a shitass day. Every inch of it
hot and miserable. First off, Nadine at the Blue Chip
got some sorta sick, so that Mongoloid boy of hers
was workin' the grill. That fuckin' idiot don't know
rat shit from Rice Krispies. I ate breakfast at nine, was
pukin' up pigs in a blanket like a sick dog by ten
thirty.

PETE

Isn't there a law or something against retards serving
food to the public?

McGRAW

Well, if there ain't, there sure oughta be. Who knows
what goes on inside a Mongoloid's mind?

PETE

You could sue the shit outta her, ya know. That kid
belongs under a circus tent, not flippin' burgers. You
could own that fucking place.

McGRAW

What the hell would I do with that grease pit?
Besides, Nadine's got enough of a cross to bear just
taking care of that potato head. Then all this Abilene
shit happened. You heard about that bank robbery in
Abilene, didn't ya?

PETE

That's all that's been on the box all day. They killed some people, didn't they?

McGRAW

Four Rangers, three cops, and two civilians. And they took a lady bank teller as a hostage.

Pete doesn't say anything.

McGRAW

They'll probably make a run for the border, which would bring 'em this way. And if we get our hands on those shitasses, we're talkin' payback time. We'll get 'em all right. I gotta piss. I'm gonna use your commode.

PETE

Knock yourself out.

McGraw downs his last drop of beer, crushes the can, and exits into the bathroom.

The black-suited man by the beer cooler turns around and, with the prep school girl in tow, walks rapidly toward Pete. We see that the girl is crying.

BLACK-SUITED MAN #1

(to Pete)

Do you think I'm fuckin' playing with you, asshole?

(points to the tearful prep school girl)

Do you want this little girl to die?

(pointing to the blond girl by the other guy)

> Or that little girl? Or your bosom buddy with the
> badge? Or yourself? I don't wanna do it, but I'll turn
> this fuckin' store into the Wild Bunch if I even think
> you're fuckin' with me.

*The two men in black suits are the notorious Abilene bank robbers,
SETH and RICHARD GECKO, "the Gecko Brothers." And
the other customers are all being held hostage. Seth is the one with the
prep girl. Richard is with the blond.*

Everybody speaks low and fast.

PETE

What do you want from me? I did what you said.

SETH

Letting him use your toilet? No store does that.

PETE

He comes in here every day and we bullshit. He's
used my toilet a thousand times. If I told him no, he'd
know something was up.

SETH

I want that son-of-a-bitch outta here, in his car, and
down the road or you can change the name of this
place to "Benny's World of Blood."

*Richard, holding tightly the hand of the terrified girl, leans next to
Seth's ear and whispers something. Seth looks at Pete.*

SETH

Were you giving that pig signals?

PETE

What? Are you kidding? I didn't do anything!

Richard whispers something else in Seth's ear.

SETH

He says you were scratching.

PETE

I wasn't scratching!

SETH

You callin' him a liar?

Pete controls himself.

PETE

I'm not calling him a liar, okay? I'm simply saying if I
was scratching, I don't remember scratching, and if I
did scratch, it's not because I was signaling the cop,
it's because I'm fuckin' scared shitless.

Richard speaks for the first time in a low, calm voice to Seth.

RICHARD

The Ranger's taking a piss. Why don't I just go in
there, blow his head off, and get outta here.

PETE

Don't do that! Look, you asked me to act natural, and
I'm acting natural—in fact, under the circumstances, I
think I ought to get a fuckin' Academy Award for
how natural I'm acting. You asked me to get rid of
him, I'm doing my best.

SETH
    Yeah, well, your best better get a helluva lot fuckin'
    better, or you're gonna feel a helluva lot fuckin'
    worse.

The toilet FLUSHES.

                    SETH
    Everybody be cool.

Everybody goes back to what they were doing.

*McGraw steps out of the back. He appears to be unaware of the
situation.*

                    McGRAW
    Yeah, and I'm gonna be right back at it tomorrow. So
    tonight I'm gonna sit in front of the box and just
    drink booze. How much is the bottle?

                    PETE
    Six-fifty.

*Out of nowhere Richard WHIPS out his .45 automatic and
SHOOTS McGraw in the head.*

McGraw goes down screaming.

Richard stands over him and SHOOTS him twice more.

Seth charges forward.

                    SETH

(to Richard)

    What the fuck was that about?

RICHARD

(in a low monotone)

He signaled the Ranger.

PETE

(hysterical)

I didn't.

(to Seth)

You gotta believe me, I didn't!

RICHARD

(to Seth)

When they were talkin', he mouthed the words
"Help us."

PETE
You fuckin' liar, I didn't say shit!

Richard SHOOTS Pete and Pete falls down behind the counter.

Seth grabs Richard and throws him up against the wall.

SETH
What the fuck is wrong with you—

RICHARD
Seth, he did it. You were by the beer cooler with

your back turned. I was by the magazines, I could see his face. And I saw him mouth:

Richard mouths the words "Help us."

While Pete lies on the floor behind the counter bleeding from his bullet wound, he opens his floor safe and pulls out a gun from it.

Seth releases his brother.

                    SETH
        Start the car.

                    RICHARD
        You believe me, don'tcha?

                    SETH
        Shut up and start the car.

Richard walks away from Seth and crosses the counter . . .

when Pete SPRINGS up, gun in hand, and SHOOTS Richard in the hand.

Richard FALLS to his knees, howling.

Both Pete and Seth SPRAY the store with gunfire.

Seth DIVES down an aisle. He reloads.

Pete DUCKS behind the counter. He reloads.

Richard has crawled to safety behind an aisle.

The two girls have run out screaming.

SETH

(yelling)

Richie? You okay?

RICHARD

(yelling)

I'm not dead, but I'm definitely shot! I told you that bastard said, "Help us!"

PETE

(yelling)

I never said, "Help us!"

SETH

(yelling)

Well, that don't matter now, 'cause you got about two fuckin' seconds to live! Richie!

RICHARD

(yelling)

Yeah?

SETH

(yelling)

When I count three, shoot out the bottles behind
him!

RICHARD

Gotcha!

SETH

One . . . Two . . . Three.

The two brothers start FIRING toward the counter.

They HIT the bottles of alcohol on the shelf behind Pete.

*Pete is crouched on the ground as glass, debris, and alcohol RAIN
down on him.*

Seth grabs a roll of paper towels from off a shelf.

Richard keeps FIRING.

*Seth douses the paper towels with lighter fluid, sets it on fire with his
Zippo, then tosses it.*

The flaming roll of paper towels FLIES through the air.

The fireball lands behind the counter.

*The entire counter area immediately BURSTS INTO FLAMES.
Pete screams from behind the counter.*

Seth smiles to himself and stands.

Richard shakes his head in amusement and stands.

*Pete runs out from behind the counter, ENGULFED IN
FLAMES, still holding his weapon and FIRING.*

Seth and Richard hit the ground FIRING their .45's.

Pete, the human torch, FALLS like a tree into the Hostess Pastry display.

Seth and Richard rise from the rubble.

3 EXT. BENNY'S WORLD OF LIQUOR—DAY

They exit the store squabbling. The store is bursting into flames.

> SETH
>
> What did I tell you? What did I tell you? Buy the road map and leave.

> RICHARD
>
> What am I supposed to do, Seth? He recognized us.

> SETH
>
> He didn't recognize shit.

Both Seth and Richard stand on opposite sides of the car.

> RICHARD
>
> Seth, I'm telling you, the way he looked at us—you especially—I knew he knew.

They both climb in the car, Seth behind the wheel. Seth starts it up. The souped-up engine ROARS to life. We can hear Seth mumbling under the motor.

> SETH
>
> Low profile. Do you know what the words "low profile" mean?

CLOSE-UP: SETH'S FOOT PUNCHES GAS.

The Plymouth tears out of the parking lot backwards, hits the street, and speeds off down the road.

WE CRANE UP HIGH to see the car leaving a trail of dust behind it, as the store burns out of control.

OPENING CREDIT SEQUENCE.

Raunchy, honky-tonk MUSIC fills the theater.

CUT TO:

A3 EXT. TEXAS PANHANDLE—DAY

The Plymouth tears ass across Texas plains. As TITLES PLAY OVER, we see Seth and Richard enjoying their getaway/road trip. Seth, behind the wheel, pops open a bottle of prescription pills, empties out four of the red capsules in his hand, pops them in his mouth, and washes it back with a slug of Jack Daniel's from a pint bottle.

Richard looks at Seth through the hole in his hand. Like a boxer, Richard wraps up his wounded hand with gaffer's tape.

The camera leaves the boys, as they whoosh down the street, and goes along the length of the car to the trunk. It hangs on the trunk. Then we see through the trunk, like Superman:

AN OLDER WOMAN tied up and helpless in the trunk.

The rest of the titles play over black as the song continues.

CREDIT SEQUENCE ENDS

CUT TO:

4 EXT. EMMA AND PETE'S GRAVY TRAIN—DAY

Emma and Pete's Gravy Train is a truck stop off of Highway 290.

SUBTITLE APPEARS AT THE BOTTOM OF THE
SCREEN:

FORT STOCKTON
238 MILES FROM THE MEXICAN BORDER

5 INT. EMMA AND PETE'S GRAVY TRAIN—DAY

Emma and Pete's PATRONS are made up of regulars, truckers,
cowboys, and road-weary travelers. The CAMERA DOLLIES
through the maze of tables, patrons, and waitresses.

It stops when it gets to a table occupied by the FULLER FAMILY.
The Fullers definitely fall into the road-weary category. The members
of the unit consist of the father, JACOB, age 44, an ex-preacher, a
good man with rough edges, and his two children. KATE, age 19, is
a young beauty who possesses what can only be described as an apple
pie sensuality. She is dressed like a nice Christian girl, complete with
crucifix. SCOTT, age 16, is Jacob's Chinese adopted son. Scott is a
likable, long-haired kid who always wears a T-shirt with the name of
the heavy metal garage band he plays guitar for, ''Precinct 13.'' The
three of them are wolfing down a late lunch.

JACOB

We got about two more hours of daylight left. That'll
get us into El Paso, which is right next to the border.
We'll stop at a motel—

SCOTT

Stop? We're not going to actually stop at a motel, are
we?

*Scott and Kate speak together, obviously repeating something that
Jacob has said about three hundred times.*

SCOTT AND KATE

We've got a Winnebago. We don't need those
overpriced roach havens. We're self-contained.

JACOB

Okay, okay, maybe I was little overzealous, but give
me a break. I just bought it.

Scott and Kate continue the impersonation.

SCOTT

Why, just look at all this. You got your kitchen—

KATE

—you got your microwave—

SCOTT

—you got your sink—

KATE

—you got your shower—

SCOTT

—see this, television!

KATE

Feel this, real wood paneling. That's real wood, too,
not that fake stuff.

JACOB

Unless you two wiseacres wanna be introduced to the
joys of hitchhiking, what say we drop this?

SCOTT

(to Kate)

The truth hurts.

KATE

(to Scott)

It's the bitterest of pills.

JACOB

You two ought to start a stand-up act, because you're
just wasting your humor on me.

KATE

Ain't it the truth.

SCOTT

Why do you wanna stop?

JACOB

I'm exhausted.

SCOTT

Lie in the back, Dad, I'll drive us into Mexico.

Jacob gives Scott a look that says, "You aren't touching my new motor home."

JACOB
I just bet you would. Don't even think about it. Besides, I want to have one night's sleep in an honest-to-goodness bed. The beds in the home are okay, but they're not like a real bed.

KATE
Hey, if we go to a motel, we can swim.

SCOTT
I'll be right back. I'm gonna go to the bathroom.

Scott gets up from the table and walks out back to the restroom.

Jacob and Kate are left alone. There's an awkward moment of silence before . . .

KATE
Dad, when I called the machine to check out our messages, there was one from Bethel Baptist. Mr. Franklin said he wouldn't permanently replace you until we came back. He said when we come home, if you still feel the same way—

JACOB
That's very nice of Ted, but I'll call him tomorrow and tell him not to bother waiting.

KATE
I didn't want to talk about this in front of Scott because he gets upset. But don't you believe in God anymore?

JACOB

Not enough to be a pastor. Look, I know this is hard
on you kids. After Jenny's death, this is probably the
last thing you need. But I can't do it any longer. My
congregation needs spiritual leadership. Well, they
can't get that from me anymore. My faith is gone. To
answer your question, yes, I do believe in God. Yes, I
do believe in Jesus. But do I love them? No. After
Jenny died, I just thought, what's the point?

KATE

(pushing him)

It's just, all our lives you've been a pastor. For twenty
years you've preached trust in the Lord. And then one
day you wake up and say, fuck him?

JACOB

I didn't say, fuck him. I'm just not connected
anymore.

KATE

That happens, you'll get it back.

JACOB

Kate, give your old man a little credit. Every person
who chooses the service of God as their life's work
has something in common. I don't care if you're a
preacher, a priest, a nun, a rabbi or a Buddhist monk.
Many, many times during your life you'll look at your
reflection in the mirror and ask yourself, am I a fool?
We've all done it. I'm not going through a lapse.
What I've experienced is closer to awakening. I'm not

trying to shake your faith. I've just decided not to
devote my life to God anymore.

KATE

What do you think Mom would say?

JACOB

Mom's got nothing to say, she's dead.

CLOSE-UP: COUNTER BELL. A hand slams down on it.
RING.

6 INT. LOBBY—DEW DROP INN—DAY

Seth stands at the front desk of the Dew Drop Inn. A standard-issue
Texas motel. Richard sits outside in the car. Nobody responds to the
bell. Seth BANGS it impatiently five times.

TEXAS VOICE (O.S.)
Hold your horses!

An OLD-TIMER walks through a curtain behind the counter. He's
eating a BBQ rib.

OLD-TIMER

(rough)

Whatcha want?

SETH
Whatcha think I want, ya mean old bastard? I wanna
room.

7 EXT. COURTYARD—DEW DROP INN—DAY

Richard sits in the car listening to Merle Haggard on the radio. He watches from his perspective, Seth taking the keys, walking outside, and getting in the car. Seth starts it up, and drives them to their room.

RICHARD

Do they have cable?

SETH

No.

RICHARD

Do they have an X-rated channel?

SETH

No.

RICHARD

Do they have a waterbed?

SETH

They don't have anything except four walls and a roof, and that's all we need.

Their car drives up to room #9, but they park backing up the trunk close to the door.

The two brothers get out of the car.

SETH

(tossing Richie the motel keys)

Open the door. We gotta do this fast.

Richie opens the door.

Seth goes to the trunk, looks around the courtyard. It's empty.

CLOSE-UP: KEY going into the trunk lock, turning.

TRUNK POV: Seth looking into the camera.

SETH'S POV: A WOMAN in her late 40s is lying scrunched up in the trunk.

She is the HOSTAGE BANK TELLER from Abilene. She's stiff, scared, and looks an absolute mess.

> SETH
>
> Don't say a word.

The two brothers, quick as lightning, yank the woman out of the trunk and whisk her into the motel room. SETH closes the trunk, looks around for any Johnny eyewitnesses, doesn't see any, slams the door.

8 INT. SETH AND RICHARD'S ROOM—DAY

Seth turns from the door, sees the Hostage Woman standing.

> SETH
>
> You. Plant yourself in that chair.

She sits down in the chair.

> HOSTAGE
>
> What are you planning on doing with—

SETH

—I said plant yourself. Plants don't talk. You wanna get on my good side? Just sit still and don't make a peep.

She shuts up.

Richard slowly takes off his jacket. He winces from his wound.

SETH

Let me help you.

Seth helps Richard take his jacket off.

SETH

How's it feel?

RICHARD

How ya think, it hurts like a son-of-a-bitch.

Richie goes over to the bed and lies down on it. Seth takes the pillows and stacks them for Richie to prop his back up against.

SETH

I got both rooms on either side of us, so we don't gotta worry about eavesdropping assholes. How's that feel? You okay?

RICHARD

Feels good.

SETH

I'm gonna go get the money.

He heads for the door.

9 EXT. COURTYARD—MOTEL—DAY

*Seth goes into the car, takes out a big suitcase. He scans the perimeter
with his eyes, goes back inside.*

10 INT. MOTEL ROOM #9—DAY

*Seth comes back in, lays the suitcase on the bed. Richie has the TV
remote control in his hand and he's flipping stations. Seth looks at his
watch.*

SETH
It's about five o'clock.

(to Hostage)

What time does it get dark around here?

HOSTAGE
About seven.

SETH
Good. I'm going toward the border to check things
out while it's still daylight. Call Carlos and arrange the
rendezvous.

RICHARD
Hey, when you talk to him, see if you can arrange a
better deal than thirty percent.

SETH
That's their standard deal, brother. They ain't about to
change it for us.

RICHARD

Did you even try to negotiate?

SETH

These guys ain't spic firecracker salesmen from
Tijuana. They don't even know the meaning of the
word "barter." You wanna stay in El Ray? You give
them thirty percent of your loot. It's scripture. So it is
written, so shall it be done. You want sanctuary, you
pay the price, and the price is thirty percent.

RICHARD

All I'm saying—

SETH

—This conversation is over.

*Richie shrugs and turns back to the TV. Seth turns to the Hostage,
grabs a chair, and slides it up in front of her.*

SETH

Now, we need to have a talk. What's your name?

HOSTAGE

Gloria.

He shakes her hand.

SETH

Hello, Gloria, I'm Seth and that's my brother Richie.
Let's cut to the chase. I'm gonna ask you a question
and all I want is a yes or no answer. Do you want to
live through this?

GLORIA

Yes.

SETH

Good. Then let me explain the house rules. Follow
the rules, we'll get along like a house on fire. Rule
number one: No noise, no questions. You make a
noise . . .

(he holds up his .45)

Mr. Forty-five makes a noise. You ask a question, Mr.
Forty-five answers it. Now, are you absolutely,
positively clear about rule number one?

GLORIA

Yes.

SETH

Rule number two: You do what we say, when we say
it. If you don't, see rule number one.

*Seth takes the .45, places the barrel next to the woman's cheek. She
squirms and shuts her eyes. He pulls back the hammer.*

SETH

Rule number three: Don't you ever try and fuckin'
run on us. 'Cause I got five little friends, and they all
run faster'n you can. Got it?

She nods her head yes.

He takes the gun away and replaces the hammer.

SETH

Open your eyes.

She does.

> SETH

Gloria, you hang in there, follow the rules, and don't
fuck with us, you'll get out of this alive. I give you
my word. Okay?

She nods her head yes.

Seth rises.

> SETH

I'll be back in a bit.

He exits.

*Richard looks to the TV, then looks to Gloria sitting across the room
in the chair.*

> RICHARD

Wanna come up here on the bed and watch TV with
me?

You can tell she doesn't want to.

He pats the empty space next to him.

> RICHARD

Come on.

*She gets out of her chair, walks across to the bed, and sits next to
him.*

11 EXT. PHONE BOOTH—DAY

A phone booth outside of a gas station. Seth is in the middle of a conversation with the party on the other end.

SETH
Things are real hot here. Crossing's gonna be a bitch.

(pause)

Don't worry, we'll get across. But when we do, where do we go?

(pause)

Can we make it as close to the border as possible? Texas wants our balls. The quicker we're in your protection, the better I'll feel.

(pause)

Okay, where?

(pause)

The Titty Twister?

(he laughs)

I love it already. Okay, Carlos, I'll see you and your men at the "Titty Twister" tomorrow morning.

(pause)

Bye, my friend.

Seth hangs up the phone, lights up a cigarette with his Zippo lighter, and exits frame. After Seth exits, leaving the frame empty, a subtitle appears:

EL PASO
5 MILES FROM THE MEXICAN BORDER

CUT TO:

12 INT. SETH AND RICHARD'S MOTEL ROOM—
NIGHT

Richard lies on the bed by himself, propped up by pillows, watching TV.

ON TV

A local newscaster named KELLY HOUGE is reporting a story about the brothers.

KELLY HOUGE

(talking to camera)

> This bloody crime spree started just a week ago today.
> The oldest of the two brothers . . .

MUG SHOT OF SETH

KELLY HOUGE (V.O.)
. . . Seth Gecko was serving time in Rolling's Kansas
State Penitentiary for his part in the 1988 Scott City

bank robbery in which two law enforcement officers lost their lives.

BACK TO KELLY

> **KELLY HOUGE**
> Having served eight years of his twenty-two-year sentence, Seth Gecko was brought to Wichita Municipal Courthouse for his first parole hearing. It was while at the courthouse that this man . . .

MUG SHOT OF RICHARD GECKO

> **KELLY HOUGE (V.O.)**
> . . . his younger brother Richard Gecko, a known armed robber and sex offender, pulled off a daring daylight escape . . .

BACK TO KELLY

> **KELLY HOUGE**
> . . . resulting in the death of four Wichita law enforcement officers, and this woman . . .

PHOTO OF WOMAN SMILING

> **KELLY HOUGE (V.O.)**
> . . . Heidi Vogel, sixth-grade teacher, who was run over by the Geckos during a high-speed pursuit through downtown Wichita.

MAP OF AMERICA

A red line travels from Wichita to Oklahoma.

KELLY HOUGE (V.O.)
From there the brothers traveled from Kansas through
Oklahoma . . .

The red line enters Texas and the camera moves into Texas.

KELLY HOUGE (V.O.)
. . . into the great state of Texas. And then finally . . .

WE ZOOM in on a red-circled Abilene.

KELLY HOUGE (V.O.)
. . . into Abilene.

We hear GUNFIRE and SCREAMS.

CUT TO:

V13 EXT. THE CRIMINAL COURT BUILDING—DAY

*Kelly Houge walks down the courthouse steps of the criminal courts
building of Abilene. She talks to the camera. Cops, lawyers, and
citizens bustle in the background.*

KELLY HOUGE
The list of the dead climbed up three more notches
since our last telecast.

CUT TO:

*PHOTO: OFFICER SHERMAN GOODELL in full police
uniform.*

> KELLY HOUGE (V.O.)
> Officer Sherman Goodell, who was in intensive care
> following the gun battle outside of the Valley Federal
> bank building . . .

CUT TO:

V14 EXT. COURTHOUSE—DAY

Kelly Houge standing on the courthouse steps talking into the camera.

> KELLY HOUGE
> . . . died about forty-five minutes ago at Hopkins
> General Hospital. And about six hours ago, during a
> daylight liquor store robbery in Big Springs, the
> Gecko Brothers killed another Texas Ranger . . .

CUT TO:

PHOTO: EARL McGRAW in uniform.

> KELLY HOUGE (V.O.)
> . . . Earl McGraw.

CUT TO:

PHOTO: PETE in a Hawaiian shirt holding up a big fish.

> KELLY HOUGE (V.O.)
> . . . and liquor store clerk Pete Bottoms.

CUT TO:

VIDEO FOOTAGE: Of Benny's World of Liquor burning down.

KELLY HOUGE (V.O.)

Then they proceeded to burn the store down to the ground.

CUT TO:

VIDEO GRAPHIC: Picture of the Gecko Brothers with a tally underneath:

THE GECKO BROTHERS
WICHITA JAIL BREAK
VALLEY FEDERAL BANK ROBBERY
BIG SPRINGS CONVENIENCE STORE ROBBERY

DEATH TOLL
13

TEXAS RANGERS	POLICE OFFICERS	CIVILIANS
4	7	2

KELLY HOUGE (V.O.)

That changes the death toll to fifteen.

(It changes under "Death toll")

Five Texas Rangers . . .

(it changes)

Eight police officers . . .

(it changes)

Three civilians.

(it changes)

CUT TO:

BACK TO KELLY

>   KELLY HOUGE
> And one hostage . . .

CUT TO:

PHOTO: GLORIA HILL

>   KELLY HOUGE (V.O.)
> . . . bank teller and mother of four, Gloria Hill.

KELLY TO CAMERA

>   KELLY HOUGE
> Heading the case to bring these fugitives to justice is
> FBI agent Stanley Chase. We talked with Agent
> Chase earlier this afternoon.

CUT TO:

V15 VIDEO INTERVIEW

Kelly Houge interviewing STANLEY CHASE of the FBI.

>   STANLEY CHASE
> For the time being we are very confident we will

apprehend the fugitives in the next forty-eight hours.
The Bureau, local law enforcement, and the Texas
Rangers have all joined forces in forming a dragnet to
snare Seth and Richard Gecko.

KELLY HOUGE
Agent Chase, does it appear that they are heading for
Mexico?

STANLEY CHASE
Yes, it does, Kelly. We have already alerted the
Mexican authorities. They intend to cooperate every
way possible in bringing these fugitives to justice.

KELLY HOUGE
Are you optimistic about the safety of the hostage
they took in Abilene, Gloria Hill?

STANLEY CHASE
We've received no news one way or the other. We
can only hope for the best.

KELLY HOUGE
What about the report from an eyewitness at the
liquor store who said one of the brothers was shot?

STANLEY CHASE
This can't be confirmed at this time, but we do
believe it to be true. We have reason to believe it was
the younger brother, Richard, and he was shot in the
vicinity of his neck and shoulders by the store's clerk.

KELLY HOUGE
Is it safe to assume that because of the death count

involved and the loss of life of law enforcement
officers, the Bureau, the Rangers, and the police force
are taking this manhunt personally?

                    STANLEY CHASE
I would say that's a very safe assumption.

                                        CUT TO:

16 RICHARD SMILES.

                    RICHARD

(Newscaster's voice)

       Is it safe to assume since the law enforcement
       authorities in the great state of Texas are homosexuals
       of a sick and deviate nature, that they will be too busy
       fucking each other up the ass to actually catch the
       Gecko Brothers?

(in an FBI voice)

       I would say that's a very safe assumption.

*He changes a channel on the television. We see a CASPER the
Friendly Ghost cartoon on the screen.*

                    CASPER
Would you play with me?

A big burly COP turns around.

COP

Sure, little boy . . . A GHOST!!!

The cop heads for the hills. Casper cries.

Seth enters the room carrying a six-pack of beer and two take-out bags of Big Kahuna burgers.

RICHARD

Shit, I started to get worried. Where the fuck ya been?

SETH

Sight-seein'.

RICHARD

What'd ya see?

SETH

Cops.

RICHARD

Didya look at the border?

Seth dumps the burgers on the bed. Both men pop open beers and Richard goes to town on a hamburger. Seth flips off the TV.

SETH

Yeah, I saw the border. Through binoculars from on top of a high building. That's about as close as I risked getting. What's the TV say?

RICHARD

They're going to apprehend us in forty-eight hours.

Seth sits down and takes a hit off his beer.

SETH

(to himself)

I gotta figure a way to get across that goddamn
border. Longer we fuck around El Paso our lives ain't
worth a shit.

RICHARD

Look, fuck the border. Let's just dig in and wait for
things to cool down.

SETH

Richie, it's gonna get a lot fuckin' worse before it gets
any fuckin' better. We showed our ass in Texas. We
killed Texas police officers. We killed Texas fuckin'
Rangers. They ain't gonna stop lookin' till they find
us, and when they find us, they're gonna kill us.
Texans take it very personal when ya kill their law
enforcement officers. The El Paso police have already
started a motel and hotel search for us.

RICHARD

How do you know?

SETH

I heard it on the radio. We gotta get our asses into
Mexico tonight. Carlos is gonna meet us tomorrow
morning at a rendezvous on the other side, then
Carlos and his boys will escort us to El Ray and—

Seth stops talking and looks around.

SETH

Where's the woman?

RICHARD

What?

Seth's out of his chair.

SETH

What'd ya mean, what? The fuckin' woman, the
hostage. Where the fuck is she, Richard!

RICHARD

She's in the other room.

SETH

What the fuck is she doin' there!

He goes to the door of the adjoining room.

RICHARD

Seth, before you open the door, let me explain what
happened.

*Seth stops and looks at his brother. He knows what he means. He
can't say anything, only point at his younger sibling. Then he
BURSTS OPEN the door.*

*The dead, naked body of Gloria Hill lies on the bed. It's obvious
Richard raped her and killed her.*

*Seth covers his eyes with his hands. He slowly enters the room with
the dead body.*

SETH

(to himself)

Oh, Richard, what's wrong with you?

Richard rises from the bed.

RICHARD

Now, Seth, before you flip out, let me just explain
what happened.

Seth slowly turns to his brother, then walks toward him.

Richard backs up.

SETH

Yeah, explain it to me. I need an explanation. What's
the matter with you?

RICHARD

(low and calm)

There's nothing wrong with me, brother. That
woman tried to escape and I did what I had to do.

SETH

No.

(pause)

That woman wouldn't of said shit if she had a
mouthful.

RICHARD

Wrong, wrong, wrong, wrong, wrong, wrong, wrong! Once you left, she became a whole different person.

SETH

(slowly approaching)

Is it me? Is it my fault?

RICHARD

It's not your fault, it's her fault!

Seth grabs Richard and THROWS him in the corner of the room, holding tightly to his wrist.

SETH

Is this my fault? Do you think this is what I am?

RICHARD

What?

SETH

This is not me! I am a professional fucking thief. I steal money. You try to stop me, God help you. But I don't kill people I don't have to, and I don't rape women. What you doin' ain't how it's done. Do you understand?

RICHARD

Seth, if you were me—

SETH

Just say yes! Nothing else, just say yes.

RICHARD

Yes.

SETH

Yes, Seth, I understand.

RICHARD

Yes, Seth, I understand.

Seth hugs his little brother. Tight.

SETH

(whispers in Richie's ear)

We get into Mexico, it's gonna be sweet Rosemary, hundred-proof liquor, and rice and beans. None of this shit's gonna matter.

17 INT. MOTOR HOME—NIGHT

Scott and Kate are in the front seat of their parked motor home. The motor home's parked in front of the Dew Drop Inn's front office. We see Jacob inside getting a room from the Old-Timer.

KATE

I can't believe he's stopping here. This place looks totally cruddy.

Jacob walks out of the office. Kate yells from the motor home:

KATE

Dad, why are we stopping here?

He opens the motor home door and climbs in.

> JACOB
>
> There's nothing wrong with this place.

> KATE
>
> It's a flop house.

> JACOB
>
> It's not a flop house. It's basic and simple. That
> doesn't make it a flop house.

> KATE
>
> If it doesn't have a pool, we're looking for a new
> place.

Starting the huge car and slowly maneuvering it through the courtyard.

> JACOB
>
> It has a bed. That's all I care about.

> KATE
>
> Other places have beds, they also have cable TV, a
> gym, room service. . . .

18 COURTYARD—NIGHT

*Seth walks out of room #9 with a beer in his hand. He's thinking
about how he's going to get over the border tonight. Lost in thought,
he steps out in the path of the Fullers' motor home.*

Jacob slams on the brakes.

Seth jumps back, startled.

Both Kate and Scott are TOSSED out of their seats onto the floor.
THUD . . . THUD . . .

KATE

Owww, my head.

Jacob (pissed) honks his horn at Seth and yells out the window:

JACOB

Watch where you're going!

THROUGH WINDSHIELD

Seth just stands right in their way without moving, gazing up at the
giant motor home.

JACOB BEHIND THE WHEEL

Kate and Scott join him up front looking at this weirdo.

SCOTT

What's this guy's problem?

JACOB

I have no idea.

Seth continues standing in their way, making no attempt to move.
Not threatening, just looking at them.

Honk!

JACOB

Anytime, man.

*The horn snaps Seth back to this world. A smile breaks out on the
escaped fugitive's face and he politely steps to one side to let them
pass.*

Pass they do!

KATE

Creepy guy.

SETH

*The Sword of Damocles is lifted from above Seth's head. He's just
solved a problem that a mere thirty seconds ago seemed unsolvable. He
knows exactly how he's going to cross the border. Whistling a happy
tune, he turns and walks back into room #9.*

19 INT. FULLERS' MOTEL ROOM—NIGHT

*The Fullers are in room #12. It's identical to the one that the Gecko
boys are in, except that the paintings above the beds are different.
Jacob has fallen asleep in his clothes on the bed.*

*Scott sits in a chair, headphones on, playing an unplugged electric
guitar. Kate is nowhere in sight.*

KNOCK . . . KNOCK . . . KNOCK . . . on the door.

Scott doesn't hear shit but his music.

Jacob stirs a bit, but doesn't wake up.

POUND . . . POUND . . . POUND . . . on the door.

Jacob SPRINGS UP. He looks over at Scott, who, lost in guitar heaven, is oblivious of the knocker, then to the door.

JACOB

(yelling)

What?

From the other side of the door comes a friendly voice.

VOICE (O.S.)
I'm your neighbor in room 9. I hate to disturb you, but I'd like to ask a favor.

Jacob swings his feet to the floor, stands up, and walks to the door. As he passes Scott, he says, in his direction—

JACOB
I hope none of this is disturbing you.

Scott can't hear him, but when he sees his dad look at him, he smiles.

Jacob opens the door and sees . . .
. . . Richard Gecko standing in the doorway, looking like the nicest guy in the entire world.

RICHARD
Hi there, I'm from room 9, my name is Don Cornelius. No, not the Don Cornelius from Soul Train. Me and my lady friend need some ice and we don't seem to have an ice bucket. Could we possibly borrow yours? I'll bring it right back.

JACOB

(still partially asleep)

Sure.

We follow Jacob as he turns to the dresser to get the motel ice bucket. He grabs it, turns back to the door, takes a couple of steps toward it, then stops in his tracks.

He sees Richard and Seth both inside the room with the door closed, both with .45's in their hands, both aimed at him.

JACOB

What is this?

Seth SLUGS Jacob in the mouth, KNOCKING him to the ground.

SETH

It's called a punch.

Scott suddenly becomes aware of what's going on around him and instinctively stands. Richard shoves his .45 in Scott's mouth.

RICHARD

Sit down.

Scott lowers himself back down onto his seat.

RICHARD

Good boy.

Jacob lifts his head off the floor and wipes blood away from his lip. He looks at his opponent, who stands over him.

SETH

(to Jacob)

What's your name?

JACOB

Jacob.

SETH

Okay, Jacob, get up and sit your ass down on the bed.
Make a wrong move and I'll shoot you in the face.

Jacob rises and sits on the edge of the bed.

SETH

(to Richard)

Okay, move the Jap over there.

Keeping the gun in Scott's mouth, Richard makes Scott rise . . .

RICHARD

Upsy daisy.

. . . guiding him over to the bed by his father.

*Richard removes the gun from Scott's mouth and stands next to his
brother, looking down at their two hostages.*

SETH

(to his hostages)

What's the story with you two? You a couple of fags?

JACOB

He's my son.

SETH

How does that happen? You don't look Japanese.

JACOB

Neither does he. He looks Chinese.

SETH

Oh, well, excuse me all to hell.

JACOB

What's this about, money?

SETH

It's about money, all right, but not yours. You see, me and my brother here are in a little hot water and we need your assistance.

The door to room #12 opens and a dripping-wet, bikini-clad Kate walks in.

The brothers spin their guns in her direction.

Kate, startled, screams.

Jacob and Scott get on their feet and move forward.

Seth spins back toward the two men, gun ready to spit.

SETH

(to Scott and Jacob)

Stop!

Jacob and Scott freeze.

Richard moves like quicksilver, shutting the door and positioning himself behind the terrified Kate.

KATE

What's going on?

RICHARD

We're having a wet bikini contest, and you just won.

JACOB

(to Kate)

It's okay, honey. Everything's going to be all right.

SETH

Just listen to Daddy, sugar, and don't do nothin' stupid.

(He turns to Jacob and Scott, who are still standing)

You two, Simon says sit the fuck down!

They slowly sit.

Richard can't take his eyes off the dripping-wet Kate.

Both Jacob and Seth see this and neither men like it. Each for their own reasons.

SETH

(to Jacob)

Where are the keys to the motor home?

JACOB

On the dresser.

SETH

Richie, take the keys. Start that big bastard up, and drive it up front.

Richard doesn't move from his position behind Kate.

Kate feels his eyes on her.

She slowly turns and looks at him.

He looks in her face.

CLOSE-UP KATE

She smiles at him.

KATE

Richie, will you do me a favor and eat my pussy?

CLOSE-UP RICHARD

RICHARD

Sure.

SETH (O.S.)

Richard!

Richard's eyes go to Seth.

Everybody is where they were. Kate never turned around.

SETH

Not when you get around to it; now.

Without saying a word, he takes the keys and leaves the room.

SETH

(pointing at Kate)

You, Gidget, go in the bathroom and put on some
clothes.

She grabs some clothes from the floor and moves toward the bathroom.

Seth GRABS her wrist.

SETH

You got three minutes. One second longer, I shoot
your father in the face. Do you understand what I just
said?

KATE

Yes.

SETH

Do you believe me?

KATE

Yes.

SETH

You damn well better. Go.

She goes into the bathroom.

JACOB

Look, if you want the motor home, just take it and
get out.

Seth grabs a chair and slides it up to his two male hostages.

SETH
Sorry, Pops, it ain't gonna be that easy.

We hear the motor home "HONK" twice outside.

SETH
Get ready to move out, we're all going on a little ride.

Jacob shakes his head no.

JACOB
Not a chance.

SETH
Come again?

JACOB
If you're taking people, take me. But my kids aren't going anywhere with you.

SETH
Sorry, I need everybody.

JACOB
My children are not going with you, and that's that.

SETH

(angry)

That's not fuckin' that . . .

(holds up his gun)

. . . this is fuckin' this.

(He calms down and looks at Scott)

Go sit over there.

Scott gets up and walks to the other side of the room, leaving the two men alone. Seth speaks in a quiet, conversational tone.

SETH
I ain't got time to fuck around with you, so I'll make this simple. Take your kids and get in the car, or I'll execute all three of you right now.

(He cocks the gun and puts it right in Jacob's face)

What's it gonna be, yes or no answer?

Jacob looks at him.

JACOB
Yes.

SETH
Good.

(to Scott)

Your old man's all right, he just saved your life.

Seth BANGS on the bathroom door.

SETH
Time's up, Princess.

The bathroom door opens. Kate stands there, wearing a T-shirt, jeans, and bare feet.

SETH

Okay, ramblers, let's get to rambling.

20 EXT. HIGHWAY—NIGHT

The motor home with the powder-keg interior drives through the Lone Star night.

21 INT. MOTOR HOME—NIGHT

Richard's in the back bed area with a gun trained on Kate and Scott. The two scared siblings hold hands.

KATE

Excuse me.

Richard zeros in on her.

RICHARD

What?

KATE

Where are you taking us?

RICHARD

Mexico.

KATE

What's in Mexico?

RICHARD

Mexicans.

He doesn't smile.

In the front part of the motor home, Jacob sits behind the wheel, driving into the night. Seth sits in the passenger seat, going through Jacob's wallet and talking to him calmly.

SETH

(reading his driver's license)

> Jacob Fuller. Jacob, that's biblical, ain't it? What am I askin' for, of course it is.

(motioning behind him)

> What are their names?

JACOB

Scott and Kate.

Seth repeats the names as he thumbs through the wallet.

SETH

> Scott and Kate . . . Kate and Scott . . . Scott Fuller . . . Kate Fuller . . .

Seth comes to a snapshot of Jacob and his wife.

SETH

Who's this?

JACOB

My wife.

SETH
Where is the little lady?

                    JACOB
In heaven.

                    SETH
She's dead?

                    JACOB
Yes, she is.

                    SETH
How'd she die?

                    JACOB
Auto wreck.

                    SETH
Come on, gimme some more details. How'd it
happen? Some fuckin' drunk kill her?

                    JACOB
No. It was a rainy night, the brakes on the car weren't
great. She had to stop suddenly. She slid on the road,
she crashed, she died.

                    SETH
Died instantly?

                    JACOB
Not quite. She was trapped in the wreck for about six
hours before she passed on.

SETH

Whewww! Those acts of God really stick it in and
break it off, don't they?

JACOB

Yes they do.

Seth looks back at the wallet. He sees Jacob's minister's license.

SETH

Is this real?

JACOB

Yes.

SETH

I've seen one of these before. A friend of mine had
himself declared a minister of his own religion. A way
to fuck the IRS. Is that what you're doing, or are you
the real McCoy?

JACOB

Real McCoy.

SETH

You're a preacher?

JACOB

I was a minister.

SETH

Was? As in not any more?

JACOB

Yes.

SETH

Why'd ya quit?

JACOB

I think I've gotten about as up close and personal with
you as I'm gonna get. Now if you need me like I
think you need me, you're not gonna kill me 'cause I
won't answer your stupid, prying questions. So, with
all due respect, mind your own business.

SETH

I seem to have touched a nerve. Don't be so sensitive,
Pops, let's keep this friendly. But you're right, enough
with the getting to know you shit. Now, there's two
ways we can play this hand. One way is me and you
go round an' round all fuckin' night. The other way
is, we reach some sort of an understanding. Now, if
we go down that first path, at the end of the day, I'll
win. But we go down the second, we'll both win.
Now, I don't give a rat's ass about you or your fuckin'
family. Y'all can live forever or die this second and I
don't care which. The only things I do care about are
me, that son-of-a-bitch in the back, and our money.
And right now I need to get those three things into
Mexico. Now, stop me if I'm wrong, but I take it you
don't give a shit about seeing me and my brother
receiving justice, or the bank getting its money back.
Right now all you care about is the safety of your
daughter, your son, and possibly yourself. Am I
correct?

JACOB

Yes.

SETH

I thought so. You help us get across the border
without incident, stay with us the rest of the night
without trying anything funny, and in the morning
we'll let you and your family go. That way everybody
gets what they want. You and your kids get out of
this alive and we get into Mexico. Everybody's happy.

JACOB

How do I know you'll keep your word?

SETH

Jesus Christ, Pops, don't start with this shit.

JACOB

You want me to sit here and be passive. The only
way being passive in this situation makes sense is if I
believe you'll let us go. I'm not there yet. You have
to convince me you're telling the truth.

SETH

Look, dickhead, the only thing you need to be
convinced about is that you're stuck in a situation
with a coupla real mean motorscooters. I don't wanna
hafta worry about you all fuckin' night. And I don't
think you wanna be worrying about my brother's
intentions toward your daughter all night. You notice
the way he looked at her, didn't ya?

JACOB

Yes.

SETH

Didn't like it, did ya?

JACOB

No, I didn't.

SETH

Didn't think so. So, as I was saying, I'm willing to
make a deal. You behave, get us into Mexico, and
don't try to escape. I'll keep my brother off your
daughter and let you all loose in the morning.

JACOB

You won't let him touch her?

SETH

I can handle Richie, don't worry.

The two men look at each other for some measure of trust.

Seth sticks out his hand.

SETH

I give you my word.

Seth can't help but think about the last time he gave his word.

SETH

(hand sticks out)

My word's my law. Better you not take it, and that's
just where we are, than take it and not mean it.

Jacob takes his hand, but looks right into Seth.

JACOB

If he touches her, I'll kill him. I don't give a fuck how

many guns you have, nothing will stop me from
killing him.

SETH

Fair enough. You break your word, I'll kill all of you.

(calling to the back)

Kate, honey!

KATE

Yeah.

SETH

You must have a Bible in here, don'tcha?

KATE

Yeah, we got a Bible.

SETH

Get it and bring it up here, will ya, please?

Kate goes into a drawer, pulls out a Bible, and brings it up front.

SETH

Hold it right there, sweetie pie.

(to Jacob)

Put your hand on it.

Jacob does.

SETH

Swear to God, on the Bible, you won't try to escape
and you'll get us across the border.

JACOB

I swear to God I won't try to escape and I'll do my
best to get you into Mexico.

SETH

You best better get it done, Pops.

Seth places his hand on the Bible.

SETH

I swear to God I'll let you loose in the morning. And
your daughter will be safe. And I also swear if you do
anything to fuck me up, I'll slit all your throats.

TIME CUT TO:

22 INT. MOTOR HOME—NIGHT

*Richard's in the back with Kate and Scott. Richard, expressionless,
looks at Kate's bare feet.*

SLOW ZOOM KATE'S BARE FEET

EX CLOSE-UP KATE'S TOES. They wiggle.

His eyes go to her hands.

SLOW ZOOM KATE'S HANDS

EX CLOSE-UP KATE'S FINGERS

His eyes go to her neck.

SLOW ZOOM NAPE OF KATE'S NECK

EX CLOSE-UP KATE'S ADAM'S APPLE. She swallows.

His eyes move up.

SIDE PROFILE OF KATE, SLOW ZOOM TO KATE'S LIPS

Back to Richard.

> RICHARD
>
> Didya mean what you said back there?

Kate turns to him.

> KATE
>
> What?

> RICHARD
>
> In the room. Were you serious, or were you just foolin' around? I'm just bringing it up, 'cause if you really want me to do that for you, I will.

> KATE
>
> Do what?

> RICHARD

(in a whisper)

> What you said to me in the room.

KATE

(whispers back)

What did I say?

RICHARD

(whisper)

You asked me if I would—

SETH (O.S.)

Richard!

RICHARD

(to Seth)

What?

Seth and Jacob.

SETH

I told you to watch those kids, I didn't say talk to
'em. You guys ain't got nothin' to say to one another.
So cut the chatter.

Richard turns to Kate.

RICHARD

(quiet)

We'll talk later.

Kate still hasn't a clue what he means.

CUT TO:

23 EXT. THE MEXICAN BORDER—NIGHT

Automobiles are lined up, waiting one by one to go into Mexico. Cop cars with their red and blue lights flashing are all over the place. Border Patrol men and police are stopping all cars. Pulling up to the end of the line is the Fullers' mobile home.

24 INT. MOBILE HOME—NIGHT

Jacob at the wheel, Seth in the passenger seat. Seth jumps up and goes into action.

SETH
Okay everybody, it's show time. Richie, take Kate in the bathroom.

Richard grabs the terrified Kate and drags her in the bathroom.

SETH
Scott, you come up front with your daddy.

Scott does. Seth, keeping low, gets behind Jacob.

JACOB
I'm telling you, don't hurt her.

SETH

As long as you're cool, she'll be cool. What're ya
gonna say?

JACOB

I don't have the slightest idea.

SETH

Well, you just keep thinkin' of that gun next to Kate's
temple.

*Seth disappears into the bathroom with Kate and Richard, closing the
door behind him.*

*Father and son are alone for the first time since this whole thing
began.*

SCOTT

What are you gonna do?

JACOB

I'm gonna try and get us across the border.

SCOTT

No, Dad, you gotta tell 'em that they're back there.

Jacob is surprised to hear Scott say this.

25 INT. BATHROOM—MOBILE HOME—NIGHT

*The bathroom, which consists of a shower, a toilet, and a small sink,
is a tight fit with three people in it.*

Richard has his back against the wall, with his arm around Kate, holding her in front of him. One hand is over her mouth, the other holds a .45 against her head.

Kate's eyes are wide with fear.

Seth stands, .45 in hand, ready to fire if the wrong person should open the door.

Everybody talks low and quiet.

> RICHARD
> This isn't gonna work.

> SETH
> Shut up. It's gonna work just fine.

> RICHARD
> I just want to go on record as saying this is a bad idea.

> SETH
> Duly noted. Now, shut up.

Everyone's quiet for a second, till Richard breaks it.

> RICHARD
>
> (to himself)
>
> They're gonna search the van.

> SETH
>
> (offhand)

As long as you don't act like a fuckin' nut, we'll be
just fine.

RICHARD

What does that mean?

SETH

(distracted)

What?

Richard lets Kate go, she quickly moves to the side.

RICHARD

You just called me a fuckin' nut.

SETH

No, I didn't.

RICHARD

Yes, you did. You said as long as I don't act like a
fuckin' nut, implying that I've been acting like a
fuckin' nut.

SETH

Take a pill, kid. I just meant stay cool.

RICHARD

You meant that, but you meant the other, too.

Kate can't believe what she's watching.

Neither can Seth.

SETH

(serious as a heart attack)

This ain't the time, Richard.

RICHARD

(his voice rising)

Fuck those spic pigs! You called me a fuckin' nut, and where I come from, that stops the train on its tracks.

SETH

(real quiet and violent)

Keep your voice down.

RICHARD

(quiet back)

Or what?

26 BACK TO JACOB AND SCOTT

JACOB

Have you forgotten about your sister?

SCOTT

They're gonna kill us. They get us across the border, they're gonna take us out in the desert and shoot us.

JACOB

If they get over the border, they're gonna let us go.

SCOTT

Dad, I watch those reality shows. They never let anybody go. Any cop will tell you, in a situation like this, you get a chance, you go for it. This is our chance.

JACOB

What about Kate?

SCOTT

Richie is gonna rape and kill Kate before the night's over. At least now with all these cops she's got a fighting chance.

JACOB

Seth wouldn't let him do that. He gave me his word.

SCOTT

Oh, why didn't you say that, I feel so much better. Seth's a killer, a thief, and a kidnapper, but I'm sure he's not a liar.

JACOB

Son, it may not seem like it, but I know exactly what I'm doing. You're going to have to trust me on this.

SCOTT

If trusting you means trusting those fuckin' killers, I can't do that. If you don't tell the cops, I will.

Jacob grabs Scott by the front of his shirt and yanks him to him.

JACOB

Now, you listen to me. You ain't gonna do a
goddamn fucking thing, you hear me! Nobody cares
what you think, I'm running this show, I make the
decisions.

SCOTT

He's running the show.

JACOB

I'm running the show. I make the plays, and you back
the plays I make. Stop thinking with your fucking
balls. Kate in a room with a couple of desperate men
with nothing to fucking lose ain't the time to "go for
it." I need your cover. Cover my ass.

There's a HONK behind them.

They both look out the window.

It's their turn with the BORDER PATROL GUARDS.

JACOB takes the wheel and drives up.

A stern BORDER GUARD approaches JACOB's window.

BORDER GUARD

How many with you?

JACOB

Just my son and I.

BORDER GUARD

What is your purpose in Mexico?

JACOB

Vacation. I'm taking him to see his first bullfight.

27 BACK TO BATHROOM

RICHARD

I'm curious. What was the nuttiest thing I did?

SETH

This ain't the time.

RICHARD

Oh, I know, was it possibly when your ass was rotting in jail and I broke it out? Yeah, you're right, that was pretty fuckin' nutty. Not to mention stupid. But you know what? I can fix that right now.

SETH HAULS off and PUNCHES Richard smack in the head.

Richard HITS the floor.

28 GUARD AND JACOB

Guard, Jacob, and Scott hear Richard fall in the bathroom.

BORDER GUARD

What was that?

JACOB

Oh, that's just my daughter in the bathroom.

BORDER GUARD
You said it was just you and your son.

JACOB
I meant me, my son, and my daughter.

CLOSE-UP BORDER GUARD

BORDER GUARD
Open the door. I'm coming aboard.

29 BACK TO BATHROOM

CLOSE-UP KATE

We can only see Kate's face. It's scared. We hear rustling around the bathroom, but we don't know what it is.

Then it's quiet. Then we hear talking outside the door, but we can't make it out. Then we hear a knock.

KATE
I'm in the bathroom.

BORDER GUARD (O.S.)
It's the Border Patrol. Open up.

KATE
It's open.

We hear the door open and see the light change on Kate's face. She's looking up.

BORDER GUARD *in the doorway looking in.*

HE SEES: *Kate by herself, pants around her ankles, sitting on the toilet.*

KATE

Do you mind? Shut the fucking door.

BORDER GUARD

Excuse me.

He closes the door.

Kate lets out a breath.

We wait a beat. Seth pulls back the curtain in the shower; we see Richie on the floor of the shower knocked out.

Seth and Kate meet eyes.

He gives her the okay signal.

CUT TO:

BACK WINDOW MOTOR HOME

We see through the back window of the motor home, the border getting smaller as we drive away from it.

Scott knocks on the bathroom door.

SCOTT

It's clear.

Seth BURSTS out of the bathroom.

SETH

Goddamn, that was intense!

Seth goes to the back window. He sees the border getting farther and farther away. No cars following.

SETH

(to himself)

We did it.

(pause)

We're in Mexico.

Seth throws his head back and SCREAMS for joy.

Kate, emerging from the bathroom, reacts to Seth's scream, along with Scott.

Seth is so happy that he does a little jig in the back of the van.

Everybody else is still tense as shit. But Seth lets go of all his tension and becomes a new man before our eyes. He turns to Kate.

SETH

(loud and happy)

Come here, Kate!

Kate, nervous, takes a step back.

He charges for her. GRABS her, hugs her around her waist, and spins her around. When he lets her go, she stumbles dizzily onto the bed.

SETH

(to Kate)

You were magnificent! You told him to shut the fucking door. I'm hiding in the shower, and I'm thinking to myself, "Did I just fuckin' hear what I just fuckin' heard?" And what does he do—he shuts the fucking door!

Kate kind of half smiles.

SETH

If I was a bit younger, baby, I'd fuckin' marry you!

Seth goes up front and slaps Jacob on the back.

SETH

I gotta hand it to ya, Pops, you raised a fuckin' woman.

Jacob doesn't share Seth's enthusiasm, but he is relieved.

JACOB

We did our part, we gotcha in Mexico. Now it's time for your part, letting us go.

SETH

Pops, when you're right, you're right, and you are right.

KATE

(suddenly brightens)

You're gonna let us go?

SETH

In the morning, darlin', in the morning, we are G–O–
N–E and you are F–R–E–E. Now, I know I put you
guys through hell, and I know I've been one rough
pecker, but from here on end you guys are in my cool
book. Scotty, help me pick Richie up, and lay him
down. Jacob, keep going on this road till you get to a
sign that says, "Digayo." When you get to Digayo,
turn this big bastard left, go on down for a few miles,
then you see a bar called the Titty Twister. From
what I hear, you can't miss it.

JACOB

Then?

SETH

Then stop, 'cause that's where we're going.

He slaps him once again on the back, and leaves to attend to Richard.

CUT TO:

31 CLOSE-UP RICHARD without glasses, unconscious.
Seth slaps his face.

SETH (O.S.)
C'mon, kid, wake up. Don't make a career out of it.

Richard starts coming to and opens his eyes.

Seth sits at the foot of the bed.

                    SETH

   You okay?

                    RICHARD

(disoriented)

      Yeah, I think so. What happened?

                    SETH

      I don't know, you just passed out.

                    RICHARD

   I did?

                    SETH

      Yeah, we were just standing there. You said
      something about your shoulder hurting, then you just
      hit the ground like a sack of potatoes.

                    RICHARD

   Really?

                    SETH

      Yeah. When you fell, your head smacked the toilet
      hard. It scared the shit outta me. Sure you're okay?

                    RICHARD

      Yeah, I guess. I'm just a little fucked up.

                    SETH

      Well, let me tell ya something, gonna clear your head
      right up. We are officially Mexicans.

RICHARD

What?

SETH

We are . . .

(singing)

"South of the border down Mexico way."

RICHARD

We are?

SETH

Yep. We're heading for the rendezvous right now.
We get there, we pound booze till Carlos shows up,
he escorts us to El Ray. And then me and you,
brother, kick fuckin' back. How ya like them apples?

Slowly shaking the cobwebs out of his head:

RICHARD

Far out.

(pause)

Where are my glasses?

SETH

They broke when you fell.

RICHARD

Oh, fuck, Seth, that's my only pair!

SETH

Don't worry about it, we'll get you some glasses.

RICHARD

Whatdya mean, don't worry about it. Of course I'm
gonna worry about it, I can't fuckin' see.

SETH

When we get to El Ray, I'll take care of it.

RICHARD

Yeah, like a Mexican hole-in-the-wall's gonna have
my fuckin' prescription.

SETH

It's not a big deal, unless you make it a big deal. Now,
I'm real happy, Richie, stop bringing me down with
bullshit.

Jacob calls to the back.

JACOB

Guys! We're here.

CUT TO:

32 A neon sign that flashes:

"*THE TITTY TWISTER*
BIKER/TRUCKER BAR, DUSK TILL DAWN"

*Underneath the joint's proud name on the sign, and on top of
"Biker/Trucker bar, Dusk till Dawn," is a well-endowed woman,
whose breast is being twisted by a neon hand.*

33 EXT. THE TITTY TWISTER—NIGHT

The neon sign sits on top of the rudest, sleaziest, most crab-infested, strip joint, honky-tonk whorehouse in all of Mexico.

The Titty Twister is located out in the middle of nowheresville. It sits by itself with nothing around it for miles. A plethora of choppers and eighteen wheelers are parked out in front. The walls almost pulsate from the LOUD, RAUNCHY MUSIC within the structure. Signs cover the walls outside reading things like: "NUDE DANCING," "WHORES," "BEER," "AUTHENTIC MEXICAN FOOD," "BIKERS AND TRUCKERS ONLY," "OPEN DUSK TILL DAWN," "THURSDAY COCKFIGHT NIGHT," "WEDNESDAY DOGFIGHT NIGHT," "DONKEY SHOW MONDAYS," "EVERY FRIDAY BARE KNUCKLE FIGHT TO THE DEATH, FEATURING THE LOVELY SANTANICO PANDEMONIUM," "DANNY THE WONDER PONY," and "THE SLEAZY TITTY TWISTER DANCERS."

In the parking lot, a BIKER and a TRUCK DRIVER beat the shit out of each other, one with a pipe, the other with a hammer. A SECOND BIKER fucks a Titty Twister WHORE against the wall. A greasy man, known as CHET PUSSY, stands in the parking lot, soliciting customers through a Mr. Microphone.

CHET

Pussy, pussy, pussy! All pussy must go. At the Titty Twister we're slashing pussy in half! This is a pussy blow-out! Make us an offer on our vast selection of pussy! We got white pussy, black pussy, Spanish pussy, yellow pussy, hot pussy, cold pussy, wet pussy, tight pussy, big pussy, bloody pussy, fat pussy, hairy pussy, smelly pussy, velvet pussy, silk pussy, Naugahyde

pussy, snappin' pussy, horse pussy, dog pussy, mule
pussy, fake pussy! If we don't have it, you don't want
it!

The Fullers' recreational vehicle pulls into the parking lot and stops.

34 INT. MOTOR HOME—NIGHT

*What's left of the Fuller family and the Gecko family look out the
windshield onto the sight that is the Titty Twister.*

SETH

(to the group)

Okay, troops, this is the home stretch. Here's the deal;
this place closes at dawn. Carlos is gonna meet us here
sometime before dawn. Which by my guesstimate is
somewhere between three or four hours from now.
So we're gonna go in there, take a seat, have a
drink—have a bunch of drinks—and wait for Carlos.
That could be an hour, that could be three hours, I
don't know which. But when he gets here, me and
Richie are going to leave with him. After we split,
you guys are officially out of this stew pot. Let me just
say I'm real happy about where we're at. We got a
real nice, "I don't fuck with you—you don't fuck
with me" attitude going on. Now, if everybody just
keeps playin' it cool—and I'm talking to you, too,
Richie—everybody's gonna get what they want.
Comprende, amigos?

Everybody nods and mutters in agreement.

> SETH
>
> Okay, hard drinkers, let's drink hard. I'm buyin'.

35 EXT. PARKING LOT—NIGHT

The camper door FLIES OPEN and the two brothers and the Fuller family step out into the night.

They look across the parking lot at the Titty Twister. It literally looks in some ways like the entrance to hell.

> JACOB
>
> Out of the stew pot and into the fire.

> SETH
>
> Shit, I been to bars make this place look like a fuckin' 4-H club.

> RICHARD
>
> I gotta say I'm with Jacob on this. I been to some fucked up places in my time, but that place is fucked up.

Seth can't believe it.

> SETH

(in a baby-talk voice)

> Awww, whatsa matter, is the little baby too afraid to go into the big scary bar?

The two brothers square off, not like strangers fighting, but like brothers fight. They talk real quiet but real personal.

                    RICHARD
That's what you think?

                    SETH
That's how you're lookin', Richie.

                    RICHARD
I'm lookin' scared?

                    SETH
That's what you look like.

                    RICHARD
You know what you look like?

                    SETH
No, Richie, what do I look like?

                    RICHARD
You're lookin' green.

That's not what Seth expected to hear.

                    SETH
How?

                    RICHARD
Where are you right now?

                    SETH
What do you mean?

RICHARD

Where are you?

SETH

I'm here with you.

RICHARD

No, you're not. You're sippin' margaritas in El Ray.
But we're not in El Ray. We're here—getting ready
to go in there. You're so pleased with yourself about
getting into Mexico, you think the job's down. It
ain't. Get back on the clock. That's a fuck-with-you
bar. We hang around there for a coupla hours, in all
likelihood, we'll get fucked with. So get your shit
together, brother.

SETH

My shit is together.

RICHARD

It don't look together.

SETH

Well, it is. Just because I'm happy doesn't mean I'm
on vacation. You're just not used to seein' me happy,
'cause it's been about fifteen fuckin' years since I been
happy. But my shit is together.

Richard looks at him.

RICHARD

Okay . . . I'm gonna believe you.

SETH

You better believe me.

RICHARD

Now, I don't better do nothin'. I wanna believe you.
But I'm watchin' you.

SETH

You'll see somethin'.

RICHARD

What'll I see?

SETH

You'll see how it's done.

RICHARD

Well, that's what I wanna see.

SETH

That's what you will see.

RICHARD

Show me.

*Seth looks at Richard a moment. Holds out his fist. Richard bumps
it. Then the two brothers followed by the Fullers move to the bar.*

They walk toward the bar's entrance.

Chet Pussy talks into the microphone.

CHET

(yelling into the microphone)

Take advantage of our penny pussy sale. Buy any

piece of pussy at our regular price, you get another
piece of pussy, of equal or lesser value, for a penny.
Now try and beat pussy for a penny! If you can find
cheaper pussy anywhere, fuck it!

Chet notices our heroes, especially young Kate.

CHET

(in microphone, toward Kate)

What's this? A new flavor approaching. Apple Pie
Pussy.

SETH

Step aside, asshole.

Chet POKES HIS FINGER in Seth's CHEST.

CHET

Not so fast, Slick.

*Seth GRABS HOLD of Chet's FINGER, BENDS it
BACKWARDS till the BONE SNAPS in two.*

Chet lets out a SCREAM.

*Seth VIOLENTLY brings his HEAD FORWARD,
PULVERIZING Chet's NOSE.*

Chet FALLS to his KNEES in front of Seth.

*Seth HOOKS him with a powerful FIST UNDER his CHIN that
SNAPS Chet's HEAD BACK, and THROWS him on his
BACK.*

*After he HITS the GROUND, Seth SENDS a SAVAGE KICK
straight to Chet's FACE, ROLLING HIM OVER.*

Chet is OUT.

The whole altercation took two seconds.

Everyone's in shock and looks at Seth.

Seth looks back at Richard.

SETH
Now, is my shit together, or is my shit together?

RICHARD

(bumping fist)

Forever together!

*They head for the door. Richard stays behind for a second and gives
the fallen Chet a few, swift kicks.*

36 INT. THE TITTY TWISTER—NIGHT

*If the Titty Twister looked like the asshole of the world from the
outside, in the immortal words of Al Jolson, "You ain't seen nothin'
yet." This is the kind of place where they sweep up the teeth and
hose down the cum, the blood, and the beer at closing.*

*In the back, TOPLESS DANCERS do lap dances with customers,
while a SLEAZY SEXY STRIPPER STRIPS to RAUNCHY*

MUSIC, played at eardrum-bursting level. TWO MEN are in a savage BARE KNUCKLE FIGHT, surrounded by screaming bikers and truckers.

One of the dancers is a man with a saddle on his back; his name is DANNY THE WONDER PONY. The woman on his back, in the saddle, feet in the stirrups, hands on the reins, is VICKY, his rider. They dance around to the cheers of the crowd.

Bikers and truckers play pool in the back. Fights break out here about one every ten minutes. The customers may start 'em, but the bouncer, BIG EMILIO, ends 'em.

Seth, Richard, Jacob, Scott, and Kate walk through the door.

They each individually take in the sights and the smells.

Seth is the first to say something.

SETH
Now this is my kinda place! I could become a regular.

The man behind the bar is RAZOR CHARLIE. He eyes the group as they approach.

Their difference from the usual road waif nomads who populate the Twister disturbs him. He exchanges a knowing look across the room with Big Emilio, as the group bellies up to the bar.

SETH

Whiskey!

RAZOR CHARLIE

(in English)

You can't come in here.

SETH

Whatdya mean?

RAZOR CHARLIE

This is a private club. You're not welcome.

SETH

Are you tellin' me I'm not good enough to drink here?

RAZOR CHARLIE

This bar is for bikers and truckers only.

(points his finger to Seth)

You, get out!

Big Emilio almost magically appears behind Seth and places HIS BIG BEEFY SAUSAGE-FINGERED HAND HARD on Seth's shoulder.

BIG EMILIO

(to Seth in Spanish)

Walk, Pendaho.

Seth slowly turns his eyes to the big hand on his shoulder.

SETH

(low)

Take your hand off me.

BIG EMILIO

(Spanish)

I'm going to count to three.

SETH

No, I'm going to count to three.

BIG EMILIO

Uno . . .

SETH

Two . . .

Jacob jumps in the middle.

JACOB

Now wait a minute, there's no reason to get ugly.
There's just a misunderstanding going on here. You
said this bar is for truckers and bikers. Well, I'm a
truck driver.

Everybody looks at Jacob.

As Jacob talks he takes out his wallet.

JACOB

If you look outside your door, parked in your parking
lot, you'll see a recreational vehicle. That's mine. In
order to drive that legally, you need a class-two
driver's license. That is the same license that the DMV
requires truck drivers to carry in order to drive a
truck.

(He takes the license out of his wallet and lays it on the bar)

> That is me, and this is my class-two license. This is a
> truck driver's bar, I am a truck driver, and these are
> my friends.

Everybody's a little stunned after Jacob's speech.

*Razor Charlie picks up the license, looks at Jacob, looks at everyone
in the party, and smiles.*

RAZOR CHARLIE

(to Jacob)

> Welcome to the Titty Twister. What can I get you?

Seth BRUSHES OFF Big Emilio's paw.

SETH
Bottle of whiskey and five glasses.

*Razor Charlie's eyes go to Seth. Even though he has a big smile on
his face, he looks like he's going to kill Seth. But instead he just says,*

RAZOR CHARLIE
Coming right up.

Razor Charlie goes for the bottle.

Big Emilio gives the party one last look and walks away.

Richard gives Jacob a buddy punch on the shoulder.

RICHARD
        Good job, Pops.

Seth's still frying an egg on his head.

                     SETH
        That's just fuckin' typical. Biggest number one
        problem with Mexico, it's not service-oriented. I was
        feelin' so good, and those fuckin' spics brought me
        down.

Richard puts his arm around Seth.

                    RICHARD
        Fuck 'em, shake it off.

Razor Charlie brings the bottle and the glasses.

Seth looks at the guy, still pissed.

                     SETH
        You serve food, Jose?

*Razor Charlie knows Seth's taunting him with a racial slur. But he
just smiles and says,*

                  RAZOR CHARLIE
        Best in Mexico.

                     SETH
        I kinda doubt that. We're grabbin' a table, send over a
        waitress to take our order.

Seth walks away, and the group follows him.

We just hang on the evil wheels turning inside of Razor Charlie's head.

The five of them move across the floor to a table. As they walk, Kate attracts stares, wolf whistles, and rude comments from some of the patrons. Jacob keeps near his daughter.

The dancers do their sexy routines. A big-chested, wild-haired blonde catches Scott's eye. She winks at him.

Richard leans over and whispers in Scott's ear.

RICHARD
Any time you want a lap dance with that broad, say the word. It's on me, kiddo.

He gives the boy's neck a squeeze.

Jacob's eyes survey the surroundings.

Big Emilio and Razor Charlie quietly exchange words about the party in Spanish.

RAZOR CHARLIE

(in Spanish)

They're not the usual road trash we normally feed on. But it'll be okay. No one knows they're here.

The five of them find a table and sit down.

Seth, still in a bad mood, takes the cork out of the whiskey bottle and tosses it. He pours Richie and himself a glass.

from dusk
till dawn
· 95 ·

                    SETH

Who else?

                    JACOB

Pass.

                    SETH

(picking a fight)

         Why not, against your religion?

                    JACOB

(won't be baited)

         No, I do drink, I'm just not drinking now.

                    SETH
         Suit yourself, more for me.

(to Scott)

         Scotty?

Scott shakes his head no.

                    SETH

(to Kate)

         How 'bout you?

                    KATE
         I can't. I'm not twenty-one yet.

Seth smiles.

                              SETH
          That means yes.

He pours her a drink. She looks down at it.

Seth and Richard pick up their glasses.

                              SETH
          Post time, Kate.

*Kate takes the shot glass in her hand and brings it to her lips like
she's going to take a sip.*

                              SETH
          This ain't Kentucky sipping whiskey. It's Mexican rot
          gut. You knock it down in one shot. Here we go.
          One . . . two . . . three.

*The three of them knock back the booze. Kate's whole body does a
non-drinker's tremor. Seth and Richard laugh.*

                              SETH
          That a girl.

*Jacob notices something that seems strange. All the windows in the
joint are plastered over.*

                              JACOB
          Did you notice this place doesn't have any windows?

                              SETH
          It's a strip joint whorehouse. How many windows do
          you expect it to have?

JACOB

Look, you're at where you need to be. Why don't
you let the kids go? They won't do anything while
you have me.

SETH

Shut up. I told ya what the plan was, and what it
wasn't was open to debate. Besides, these two . . .

(pointing at Scott and Kate)

. . . are safer in here with us than wandering around a
Mexican border town all night long. Just don't do
nothin' stupid and we'll all get along fine.

(to Scott)

Scotty, you sure you don't want a drink?

SCOTT

Okay, I'll have one.

JACOB

No you won't.

Seth pours Scott a shot.

SETH

Sorry, Pops, but I'm drinkin' and I don't like drinkin'
alone. Bottoms up, boy.

Scott takes the drink and he, too, experiences a non-drinker's tremor.

Seth turns to Kate.

SETH

How about you, cutie pie? Ready for round two?

KATE

Okay.

Seth just passes her the bottle. She pours her own shot and knocks it back.

RICHARD

(to Seth)

Hey, Dr. Frankenstein, I think you just created a monster.

Jacob turns to Seth and asks quietly,

JACOB

Why are you so agitated?

SETH

I'm still stewing about that ape laying hands on me. And that fuckin' bartender sticks a weed up my ass, too.

JACOB

He backed down.

SETH

He's smilin' at us. But behind his smile, he's sayin', "Fuck you, Jack." I hear that loud and clear.

JACOB

What are you going to do?

SETH

(picking up the whiskey bottle)

> I'm gonna just sit here and drain this bottle. And when I've drunk the last drop, if I still feel then the way I feel now, I'm gonna take this bottle and break it over his melon head.

JACOB

> Before we stepped in here, you told all of us to be cool. That means you, too.

SETH

(tossing it off)

> I never said do what I do, I said do what I say.

JACOB

> Are you so much a fucking loser, you can't tell when you've won?

Richard, Kate, and Scott all turn to Jacob. Nobody can believe what he just said. Neither can Seth, who calmly lays down his drinking glass.

SETH

> What did you call me?

JACOB

> Nothing. I didn't make a statement. I asked a question. Would you like me to ask it again? Very well. Are you such a loser, you can't tell when you've won?

(pause)

The entire state of Texas, along with the FBI, is
looking for you. Did they find you? No. They
couldn't. They had every entrance to the border
covered. There's no way you could get across. Did
you? Yes, you did. You've won, Seth; enjoy it.

Seth looks at Jacob, then picks up the bottle.

> SETH
> Jacob, I want you to have a drink with me. I insist.

*Jacob slides his empty glass over to Seth. Seth pours booze in Jacob's
glass and his own. Both men pick up the glasses.*

> SETH
> To your family.

> JACOB
> To yours.

They both knock 'em back and slap the empty glasses down.

> JACOB
> Now, is your shit together?

> SETH
> Forever together.

37 *Razor Charlie behind the bar grabs the greasy microphone that he uses to announce dancers.*

RAZOR CHARLIE

(announcer voice in Spanish)

> And now for your viewing pleasure: The Mistress of the Macabre. The Epitome of Evil. The most sinister woman to dance on the face of the earth. Lowly dogs, get on your knees, bow your heads, and worship at the feet of SANTANICO PANDEMONIUM!

The lights go down low.

A light hits the stage.

The opening notes of the Coaster's "Down in Mexico" fills the room.

The crowd hushes up.

And onto the stage steps SANTANICO PANDEMONIUM.

This Mexican goddess is beautiful, only not the beauty that Stendhal described in "As the Promise of Happiness," but the beauty of the siren who lures men to their doom.

She dances to the raunchy music, not like she owned the stage, but like she owned the world.

And if the patrons of the Titty Twister are her world, the world is proud to be her possession.

All activity in the bar, save Santanico, stops.

Even the Fuller/Gecko table falls under her spell.

Especially Richard, Scott, and Kate.

When the music builds to its explosive section, Santanico LEAPS from the stage, LANDING in the middle of the room.

She does an eyes-closed voodoo dance in perfect step with the beat.

As the music continues to play, a very fucked-up-looking Chet Pussy walks in. He goes over to Razor Charlie and points at Seth's table, describing what happened.

As the last verse plays, Santanico, like a snake, comes up from the ground, on top of the Fuller/Gecko table.

Richard, Kate, and Scott are enraptured.

Santanico scans the table, zeroing in on our boy Richard. She STANDS OVER him.

While moving her body to the music, she lifts up the whiskey bottle from the table, and pours the whiskey down her leg.

She lifts up her foot, with the whiskey dripping from her toes, and sticks it in Richard's face.

SANTANICO

(to Richard in Spanish)

> Drink up.

Richie, mesmerized, sucks the whiskey off her toes.

The CROWD GOES WILD.

Santanico smiles, master of all she surveys.

Jacob and Scott are embarrassed.

Kate, oddly enough, is turned on by the controlling power this woman has over a man she's deathly feared.

Seth laughs out loud—a Mexican ''yi yi yiii'' laugh.

Across the room, Razor Charlie, Chet by his side, motions over Big Emilio. He begins explaining by pointing out what Seth and company did to Chet.

Richard continues to suck her toes.

The song ends, Santanico extracts her foot from Richard's mouth. Steps off the table. Takes a drink of whiskey. Looks down at the seated Richard.

She GRABS the back of his hair, YANKS his head BACK.

His mouth OPENS because she's hurting him.

She LEANS her FACE OVER his like she's going to kiss him. Then lets the whiskey from her mouth fall into his. They never touch.

The crowd applauds.

She lets go of Richard's hair. Except for Jacob and Richard, both for their own reasons, the table applauds, none louder than Seth.

                    SETH
        Bravo! Bravo! Bravo! Now that's what I call a fuckin'
        show!

*One of Santanico's FLUNKIES brings the naked woman a robe,
which she puts on.*

Richard, still in a daze, looks up at his new friend.

SETH

(snapping his fingers)

>Earth to Richie. Don't you wanna ask your new
>friend to join us?

RICHARD

Yeah.

SETH

Well, then ask her, dumb ass.

RICHARD

(looking up at Santanico)

>*Por Favor, Señorita.* Would you care to join us?

SANTANICO

(to Richard)

>*Muy bien, gracías.*

Santanico sits down next to Richie. Seth pours her a drink.

SETH

Richie, you lucky bastard!

(to Santanico)

> Now, little lady, you could of just as easily done that
> to me. Whoa, Nelly! You got my dick harder'n
> Chinese arithmetic.

The table laughs.

SETH

> Which reminds me of a joke. Little Red Riding
> Hood is walking through the forest and she comes
> across Little Bo Peep, and Little Bo Peep says: "Little
> Red Riding Hood, are you crazy? Don't you know
> the Big Bad Wolf is walking these woods and if he
> finds you he's gonna pull down your dress and
> squeeze your titties?" Then Little Red Riding Hood
> hitches up her skirt and taps a .357 Magnum she has
> holstered on her thigh and says: "No he won't."

*As Seth tells his joke, Jacob notices Razor Charlie, Big Emilio, and
Chet moving rapidly toward their table.*

JACOB

(to himself)

> Oh, shit.

(to Seth)

> Seth—

Seth waves him away.

SETH

Not now. So finally she comes across the Big Bad

Wolf, and the Big Bad Wolf's laughing and says:
"Little Red Riding Hood, you know better than to
be walking around these woods alone. You know I'm
just gonna have to pull down your dress and squeeze
your titties." Then Little Red Riding Hood whips
out her .357, cocks it, sticks it in the Big Bad Wolf's
face and says: "No you won't. You're gonna eat me,
just like the story says."

*Seth starts laughing at his own joke uproariously. Richard, Kate,
Scott, and Santanico join in too. Before Jacob can say anything—*

The Titty Twister trio stand over the table.

RAZOR CHARLIE

(to Chet in Spanish)

Which one?

CHET

(pointing at Seth)

This piece of shit broke my finger and my nose . . .

(pointing at Richard)

. . . then this fag kicked me in the ribs while I was
down.

*That's all Big Emilio has to hear. He leans in with his beefy hand,
GRABS Richard by the shoulder.*

BIG EMILIO

(to the Gecko Brothers)

Up!

RICHARD

Fuck off, ape man!

Razor Charlie whips out a BUCK KNIFE and shoves it into Richard's wounded hand.

Seth jumps to his feet and FIRES a round from his .45 into Big Emilio, sending his bullet-ridden body to the floor.

Richard grabs the knife and stabs Razor Charlie several times, taking him to the ground.

Jacob and his children have hit the floor as well to stay out of gunfire.

The bikers, truckers, waitresses, and whores all stop what they were doing.

Richard stands in bloody triumph and stabs the wooden table with the bloody knife.

The music continues to play, though the dancers stop dancing.

Santanico, who's closest to the two brothers, smells something.

Her NOSTRILS FLARE.

Seth moves to his brother.

SETH

Are you okay?

RICHARD

Whatever.

Seth and Richard look up and see Chet still standing there.

SETH

You thought it was pretty funny, didn't you?

Both brothers FIRE on Chet.

Chet's blown left . . . right . . . left . . . right . . . then drops.

Pointing their guns toward the crowd.

SETH

Everybody be cool, or you'll be just as dead as these
fucks!

SLOW MOTION: Blood drips down Richard's hand.

SLOW MOTION: It splatters to the floor.

*The CAMERA scans the crowd. The patrons are scared, but the
waitresses, whores, and dancers lick their lips.*

*WE MOVE INTO SANTANICO'S FACE. A special aroma
fills her nostrils. Her eyes lock on Richard. The look on her face could
easily be read as intense sexual desire.*

CLOSE-UP KATE ON FLOOR

*Looks up and watches, eyes wide with fear, Santanico's
transformation.*

Her NOSE RECEDES into her face like a rodent's.

The whites of her eyes turn YELLOW.

The FANGS of a beast PROTRUDE from her mouth.

Kate yells from the floor,

> ### KATE
> Richie, look out!

Before Richie can turn around,

SANTANICO LEAPS ACROSS THE FLOOR, LANDS on his BACK, and SINKS her FANGS into Richie's neck.

Richard LETS LOOSE with an agonizing SCREAM.

Seth turns to his brother's cry.

He sees SANTANICO PANDEMONIUM, like a mongoose attached to a cobra, legs wrapped around Richard's waist, fangs buried deep in his neck, and Richard screaming and slamming about, trying to knock her off.

Richard screams to Seth:

> ### RICHARD
> Shoot her! Shoot her! Get her off!

Seth tries to aim his gun, but there's too much movement. He can't get a clear shot.

Jacob and his children can't believe what they're seeing.

Richard can't take it anymore, his knees buckle. Santanico rides him down to the floor.

Seth gets a clear shot, he takes aim and FIRES, hitting the vamp in the head, blowing her off his brother.

Richard, who's on all fours, tries to stand and gets about halfway before he stops, saying:

RICHARD

(with his dying breath)

Fucking bitch!

He tumbles over, a corpse.

SETH

Richie.

Suddenly, the eyes of Big Emilio, Razor Charlie, and Chet Pussy pop open. The "dead" men sit up with evil grins on their faces.

The patrons scream.

A WHORE locks the front door (which is a complicated lock with steel rods going into the ground), turns toward the bar, and yells:

WHORE

Dinner is served!

The bikers and truckers who have been transfixed, watching the impossible, realize that the waitresses, naked dancers, and whores they were pawing just five minutes ago have turned into yellow-eyed, razor-fanged, drool-dripping vampires.

The vamps attack.

What follows is a shark feeding frenzy.

Whores who had been sitting on customers' laps sink their teeth into unshaven necks.

Naked strippers and bikers whale the shit out of each other.

Truckers get their heads caved in by women half their size.

The patrons use whatever they can find to fend off the monsters: chairs, chair legs, broken bottles, switchblades, anything.

Jacob, Kate, and Scott make a dash and dive behind the bar. They hide and watch.

Seth stands where he was, limp dick of a .45 in his hand, too freaked, scared, and stunned to do anything. He stands motionless, watching what he can't believe.

Behind him, Santanico lies next to the dead Richard. Suddenly, his eyes POP OPEN.

She RISES in her snake/dance way.

Seth feels her and SPINS in her direction, gun raised.

SANTANICO
Let's see if you taste as good as your brother.

She approaches Seth, who FIRES at her. BAM . . . BAM . . . BAM . . . CLICK . . . CLICK . . . CLICK . . . CLICK. She laughs and gives her hair a toss back. Seth, moving backwards, is terrified.

Santanico gives Seth a SWINGING ROUNDHOUSE PUNCH to the JAW that sends him FLYING over a table, SLIDING ACROSS the FLOOR, and INTO the WALL.

A bad-ass biker named FROST, with a hideous burn on the side of his face, stands on top of a pool table, swinging a pool cue, left to right, fending off vamps.

Big Emilio picks up a biker who stabbed him with a switchblade and throws the poor bastard from one end of the bar to the other.

The biker winner of the bare knuckle fight, SEX MACHINE, goes head to head with a stripper.

The vamp might have superhuman strength, but Sex Machine has close to superhuman strength, and he's matching the vamp bitch blow for blow.

Then he GRABS her by the waist, LIFTS her up over his head, and BRINGS her DOWN HARD on an upturned table, IMPALING her on the wooden leg.

FROST is still swinging his POOL CUE, when Razor Charlie appears, straight razor in hand.

Frost JUMPS off the table to meet the challenge. Razor Charlie SWINGS at him, Frost LEAPS back, SWINGING his pool cue at him. They do this dance, till Frost CRACKS Charlie UPSIDE the HEAD with the pool cue, breaking it in half. Charlie FEELS the HIT. Frost PLUNGES the splintered end of the cue in Razor Charlie's heart.

Green blood comes out of his chest, as Charlie screams the vampire's death scream.

Seth comes to and finds Santanico standing over him. He tries to rise, but Santanico places her bare foot on his chest, pinning him down to the floor. He tries to move, but the pressure of her foot is equivalent to an engine block placed on his chest.

SANTANICO

I'm not gonna drain you completely. You're gonna turn for me. You'll be my slave. You'll live for me. You'll eat bugs because I order it. Because I don't think you're worthy of human blood, you'll feed on the blood of stray dogs. You'll be my footstool. And at my command, you'll lick the dog shit from my boot heel. Since you'll be my dog, your new name will be "Spot." Welcome to slavery.

SLOW MOTION: A WHISKEY BOTTLE FLIES THROUGH the AIR, sailing end over end.

CLOSE-UP SANTANICO

looking down at Seth, her face contorts to FEED MODE, when the bottle HITS her SQUARE in the HEAD, SHATTERING.

We see that Jacob behind the bar threw it.

Santanico, bathed in whiskey and broken glass, is momentarily dazed. She looks down at Seth.

Seth sits up, .45 in hand, and fires.

Santanico is HIT in the CHEST. The bullet from the gun makes the liquor-soaked robe ignite.

Santanico SCREAMS as she GOES UP IN FLAMES.

Big Emilio sees Santanico's fiery death. He lets out a cry.

BIG EMILIO

Noooooo!

He turns his hateful gaze on the two humans.

Seth and Jacob see Big Emilio zeroing in on them. Then they see him move his big frame in their direction. Seth turns to Jacob.

SETH
We may be in trouble.

Big Emilio walks steadily through the bar like Godzilla walks through Tokyo. Tipping over tables, knocking fighting vamps and humans alike on their asses on his way to stamp out Seth and Jacob. A TRUCKER JUMPS in his path to attack him; with a QUICK SWING of his hand the trucker is brushed aside, receiving a broken neck for the effort.

Big Emilio never breaks his stride or takes his eyes off Seth and Jacob.

Seth and Jacob both grab pieces of wood, holding it like a weapon, but the wood looks puny compared to their opponent.

Big Emilio stands in front of them.

The two men hold their wood tight.

Fangs grow in Big Emilio's mouth that make him look like a huge walking shark.

Just when Big Emilio's ready to strike, he hears behind him,

VOICE (O.S.)
Hey, you, monkey man!

Big Emilio turns and sees Sex Machine across the room.

SEX MACHINE
Anything you gotta say to them, say to me first.

Both Seth and Jacob ATTACK Big Emilio from behind. He
effortlessly knocks them away.

They both hit the ground.

Sex Machine gestures with his hand to Big Emilio to "come ahead."

Big Emilio CHARGES toward Sex Machine, like a runaway
locomotive.

Sex Machine stands his ground waiting for IMPACT.

The two huge men COLLIDE.

What follows is literally a war of the Gargantuans. The two mastiffs
POUND each other till one buckles. Finally, the one who buckles
first is Big Emilio, who HITS the floor.

Once on the floor, Seth and Jacob stand over the huge vamp,
BEATING him with clubs and pipes, like L.A.'s finest. The vamp
can do nothing except SQUIRM on the floor from the savage beating.

                    SEX MACHINE
          That's enough.

Jacob and Seth stop.

Sex Machine holds a pool cue in his hand. He SNAPS off the end
tip, making it jagged, and like a spear, STICKS it into big vamp's
fallen body. Big Emilio SCREAMS, TWITCHES, and dies. The
pool cue sticks out straight up from the dead vamp.

Chet Pussy spies Ms. Apple Pie Pussy herself, Kate. He breaks into
a lecherous grin and licks the blood from around his mouth.

Kate and Scott are cowering behind the bar when Chet appears over the top. They both let out a scream. Scott goes to protect his sister and receives a punch in the face for his trouble. Chet dives at Kate.

CHET
You know what everybody says about me? I suck!

Chet goes to bite Kate, grabbing at her T-shirt, and sees her crucifix. HE recoils backwards. Scott grabs hold of his head from behind. Kate jumps up from the floor, rips off her cross, and grabs Chet by his beatnik beard, opening his mouth. She SHOVES the cross inside. Chet's eyes roll up back into his head. Scott SLAPS Chet hard on the back.

GULP.

Chet has swallowed the crucifix. A SIZZLING sound is heard moving down from his throat to his belly. He opens his mouth and lets out a noise similar to a train whistle.

He jumps up from behind the bar, doing a wild dance from pain. He jumps from wall to wall and floor to ceiling, screaming all the while.

Kate and Scott watch him from the bar, mischievous grins on their faces.

Chet is on his knees, arms stretched out, yelling at the top of his lungs like a vamp King Lear.

CHET
I-AM-IN-AGONNNYYYY!

Chet breaks off a chair leg, muttering to himself.

CHET

Stop the pain, stop the pain, stop the pain, stop the
pain, stop the pain . . .

*He plunges the stake into his own heart, but instead of the vampire's
cry that escapes from the others upon being staked, Chet lets out a
sigh of relief.*

*By this time there are not too many people left. Most of the vampires
have been killed by wooden stakes and most of the customers have
been butchered or drained.*

*All that's left on the vampire side are two naked dancers and two
whores. On the human side are Seth, Jacob and his kids, Sex
Machine, and Frost. Aside from the children, who are hiding behind
the bar, all the humans are holding wooden stakes.*

*The four human men group together. The four female vampires
charge, teeth exposed, snarling and dripping with blood. Seth, Jacob,
Sex Machine, and Frost raise their weapons and slam, almost
simultaneously, the four vamps. All four staked bodies hit the floor.*

Kate and Scott run from behind the bar to their father's side.

*They all stand looking at the horrible carnage that has taken place.
The floor is littered with dead bodies.*

FROST

Ain't they supposed to burn up or something?

*At that moment a bright flash ERUPTS, illuminating everyone's
face. The sound of quick-burning flames fills the air. Everybody
shields their eyes from the intense light, which lasts only a split
second.*

*It vanishes, along with the bodies of the vampires. All that remains is
a smoldering mess of goo where the bodies once lay.*

*They all stare at the mess for a few seconds and then RUN for the
door. It's locked. They BANG on the door, but it's useless. It ain't
budging, yet they all go on banging.*

*. . . Except for Seth. He never ran for the door. He walks over to his
dead brother's body and kneels beside it.*

He takes his dead hand.

> SETH
> Richie, I'm sorry I fucked things up. You'd really like
> it in El Ray. We'd find peace there. I love you, little
> brother, I'll miss ya bad.

Seth goes to kiss his brother's lips when,

RICHARD'S EYES POP OPEN. They're YELLOW.

Seth RAISES his head in surprise.

> RICHARD
> I'm glad you feel that way, Seth. I love you, too.

*Richard GRABS Seth by the front of his shirt and pulls him down to
him. Fangs are now exposed. Seth tries to pull away. He
SCREAMS for the others to help. Richard PULLS Seth down to
striking distance and opens his mouth to take the big bite, when Sex
Machine grabs Seth from behind and YANKS him from Richard's
grasp. Jacob, Frost, and the kids have surrounded Richard and proceed
to KICK him and STOMP his head. Sex Machine picks up a chair
and SMASHES it against a wall. He picks up one of the chair legs*

and walks over to where the others are holding Richard down. Richard
sees the wood in the biker's hand. He knows what that means. Seth
whips out his .45 and points it at Sex Machine.

SETH
Touch my brother with that stake, biker, and
vampires won't need to suck your blood, they'll be
able to lick it up off the floor.

SEX MACHINE
He ain't your brother no more.

SETH
That's a matter of opinion, and I don't give a fuck
about yours.

Jacob, Frost, and the kids continue to hold Richard down to the
ground.

JACOB
Don't be an idiot, he'll kill us all!

Seth aims his gun at the group.

SETH
Shut up!

Richard's giggling.

RICHARD
Yeah, shut up.

Seth, still holding the outstretched gun, takes the stake out of Sex
Machine's hand. Seth lowers the .45.

SETH

Hold him down.

The smile evaporates from Richard's face.

SETH

Richie, here's the peace in death I could never give
you in life.

*Seth puts the stake over Richard's heart. Using the butt of his .45
like a hammer, he POUNDS the stake into Richard's heart. Richard
screams and dies. They all stand around the body as it BURSTS
INTO FLAMES and disintegrates into goo. Seth breaks away from
the group and walks over to the bar. He grabs a bottle of whiskey and
starts downing it. Kate, of all people, walks away from the group and
joins Seth at the bar.*

KATE

Are you okay?

SETH

Peachy! Why shouldn't I be? The world's my oyster,
except for the fact that I just rammed a wooden stake
in my brother's heart because he turned into a
vampire, even though I don't believe in vampires.
Aside from that unfortunate business, everything's
hunky-dory.

KATE

I'm really sorry.

SETH

Bullshit! You hate us. If you had half a chance you'd
feed us to them!

JACOB

Then why didn't I?

Jacob walks over to Seth.

JACOB

I saved your life. I didn't have to, but I did. And I'm
sorry you lost your brother. I'm sorry he's dead. I'm
sorry everybody's dead. Now, if we're gonna get out
of this, we need each other. And we need you sober
and thinking, not drunk and . . .

*As Jacob has been talking, a sound has started that has grown
LOUDER and LOUDER. Jacob stops in midsentence to identify it.*

JACOB

What the hell is that?

FROST

At first I just thought it was birds.

SEX MACHINE

No, it's more of a gnawing sound. Birds peck, they
don't gnaw. Rats gnaw.

Seth puts the bottle in his hand down.

SETH

It's bats.

38 EXT. TITTY TWISTER—NIGHT

*The outside of the Titty Twister is literally covered with bats,
CLAWING, FLAPPING, GNAWING, trying like hell to get
inside.*

39 INT. TITTY TWISTER—NIGHT

*Everybody listens to the bats SCRATCHING and clawing all along
the walls, the roof, and at the front door. Everyone's scared shitless
and nobody has the slightest idea what to do next. The door begins to
crack and splinter, little claws poke their way through.*

                    JACOB
         Give me a hand!

*Jacob runs to a table top. He grabs it and covers the area the bats are
trying to claw through. The others grab other items to help secure and
barricade the door.*

*As the survivors are boarding up the door and the windows in panic, a
DEAD BIKER that the vampires fed on pops open his yellow eyes.
He sits up and sees all the furious activity. Everyone's so busy they
don't notice their new friend. The dead biker vamp sets his sights on
Kate, who's putting a board into place. He springs to his feet and
POUNCES on her, just as Sex Machine turns from across the room
in her direction.*

                  SEX MACHINE
          Watch out, girly!

*The biker vamp GRABS Kate from behind. She lets out a scream.
The vamp holds her close to him in a bear hug, but she's moving*

around so much he can't get a clear bite. The others hear the scream and look toward Kate. Sex Machine, Big Emilio's baseball bat in hand, is halfway to the rescue. As the biker vamp opens his mouth to take a juicy bite out of Kate's shoulder, Kate RAMS her head back, hitting the vamp in the mouth and breaking his fangs. He releases her and spits out his teeth just as Sex Machine runs up and SWINGS the baseball bat upside the vamp's head, breaking the bat in two and sending the vamp to the floor. As the vamp lies on the floor seeing stars, Sex Machine grabs one of the broken ends of the bat and SHOVES it in the vamp's heart. He dies and bursts into flames.

At that point, three other dead victims rise to a sitting position. Sex Machine grabs a chair and THROWS it to the ground, breaking it. He grabs the four legs.

SEX MACHINE

(mumbling to himself)

Goddamn fuckin' vampires.

The biker has turned into Captain Sex Machine, Vampire Hunter. He stakes two of the vampires as they get to their feet. Both SPEW green blood, scream, die, and burst into flames. The third, a trucker vampire wearing a cat cap, SMACKS Sex Machine in the mouth, which sends the biker for a loop.

As CAT CAP runs toward the fallen Sex Machine, Kate JUMPS on his back from behind. Both of them go tumbling into a stack of whiskey cases. Sex Machine runs over and grabs Kate by the hand, pulling her up and out of the way. Cat Cap is lying in a pile of broken bottles and whiskey. Sex Machine raises his stake as Cat Cap dies and DRIVES it in the vamp's black heart. Cat Cap dies and bursts into flames, which hit the whiskey, starting a giant fire.

SEX MACHINE

Fire!

Frost and Jacob stop barricading and run to the fire.

FROST

(to Sex Machine)

We'll put this out. You stake the rest of these fuckers.

SEX MACHINE

Way ahead of ya.

(to Kate)

What's your name, girly?

KATE

Kate, what's yours?

SEX MACHINE

Sex Machine. Pleased to meet'cha. Kate, let's stake
these blood-sucker fuckers.

*Kate and Sex Machine give each other a high five and go to work
STAKING the dead bodies.*

*Jacob and FROST beat down the fire with their jackets and whatever
else is at hand.*

*A hole begins to appear where a window had been plastered over.
Little claws scrape their way through. Scott stands in front of the
window.*

SCOTT

(yelling)

We got a problem!

Seth, who is barricading doors and window, looks in Scott's direction. The hole in the plaster cracks open and out POPS a little, fleshy vampire bat/rat head. The bat/rat, which is SQUEAKING and HISSING its head off, tries to SQUEEZE its body through the newly formed hole.

Seth, gun in hand, RUNS to the window. He points the .45, point-blank range, at the head of the bat/rat.

The bat/rat sees this, makes an "oh shit" face, and YANKS his head back through the hole.

Seth was ready to fire, he lowers his gun in bewilderment, when . . .

WHAM!

The bat/rat BURSTS through the hole like shot out of a cannon, HITTING Seth in the gut and sending him FLYING, LANDING HARD on his back.

Once Seth hits the ground, the bat-thing (which has the body of a fat rat with a bat's large wingspan) lickity-split RUNS UP Seth's body to his jugular. Seth's hand GRABS the bat's neck, and tries to PUSH it away. But the bat-thing has its CLAWS DUG in Seth's clothes. The bat-thing is just inches from Seth's face. Its mouth is SNAPPING.

SETH
Get this bastard off of me!

Frost leaves Jacob with the fire, comes from behind, GRABS the bat-thing and YANKS it off of Seth.

Sex Machine and Kate are a green, bloody mess from their preventive staking of dead bodies. Sex Machine kneels by a dead body, raising the stake in his hand to spear him. The body SPRINGS UP and bites Sex Machine on the arm. Red blood squirts all over. Sex Machine screams, then brings the stake down in the body's chest. It dies, burns, and turns into goo. Sex Machine holds his bit arm and wraps it with a piece of his shirt. He quickly looks around to see if anybody saw him get bit. Nobody saw it, everybody was too busy.

Frost holds the FLAPPING, FIGHTING, SNAPPING bat-thing in front of him at arm's length. He struggles with it for awhile, then . . .

BASHES its head against the bar. The first bash takes some fight out of the little fucker, so . . . Frost BASHES its head against the bar six or seven times. He then THROWS the bat-thing on the bar, turns it over, grabs a pencil from a cup next to the register, and RAMS it in the bat-thing's heart. The bat-thing coughs and dies. There's a FLASH of FLAMES, followed by a pile of goo.

Sex Machine and Kate have covered up a hole in the plastered window with a table while Frost, Scott, and Seth wrestle with the bat-thing.

Jacob has put out the fire.

Everybody comes together, exhausted, and takes a breather. Outside, the bats continue to try and claw their way in.

JACOB

Is everybody okay?

Everyone mutters, "Yeah."

JACOB

Okay, does anybody here know what's going on?

SETH

Yeah, I know what's going on. We got a bunch of fuckin' vampires outside trying to get inside and suck our fuckin' blood! That's it, plain and simple. And I don't wanna hear any bullshit about "I don't believe in vampires" because I don't fuckin' believe in vampires either. But I do believe in my own two fuckin' eyes, and with my two eyes I saw fuckin' vampires! Now, does everybody agree we're dealin' with vampires.

Everybody agrees.

SETH

You too, preacher?

JACOB

I'm like you. I don't believe in vampires, but I believe in what I saw.

SETH

Good for you. Now, since we all believe we're dealing with vampires, what do we know about vampires? Crosses hurt vampires. Do you have a cross?

JACOB

In the Winnebago.

SETH

In other words, no.

SCOTT

What are you talking about? We got crosses all over
the place. All you gotta do is put two sticks together
and you got a cross.

SEX MACHINE

He's right. Peter Cushing does that all the time.

SETH

I don't know about that. In order for it to have any
power, I think it's gotta be an official crucifix.

JACOB

What's an official cross? Some piece of tin made in
Taiwan? What makes that official? If a cross works
against vampires, it's not the cross itself, it's what the
cross represents. The cross is a symbol of holiness.

SETH

Okay, I'll buy that. So we got crosses covered,
moving right along, what else?

FROST

Wooden stakes in the heart been workin' pretty good
so far.

SEX MACHINE

Garlic, holy water, sunlight . . . I forget, does silver do
anything to a vampire?

SCOTT

That's werewolves.

SEX MACHINE

I know silver bullets are werewolves. But I'm pretty
sure silver has some sort of effect on vampires.

KATE

Does anybody have any silver?

No.

KATE

Then who cares?

SCOTT

When's sunrise?

Jacob looks at his watch.

JACOB

About two hours from now.

KATE

So all we have to do is get by for a few more hours
and then we can walk right out the front door.

SEX MACHINE

Yeah, that's true. But I doubt our barricades, that
door, those plastered windows and these walls will last
two more hours with those bat fucks fuckin' with
'em.

JACOB

Has anybody here read a real book about vampires, or
are we just remembering what a movie said? I mean a
real book.

SEX MACHINE

You mean like a Time-Life book?

Everybody laughs.

FROST

(in a cowboy voice)

John Wesley Hardin, so mean he once shot a man for snorin'.

JACOB

I take it the answer's no. Okay then, what do we know about these vampires?

SETH

Aside from they're thirsty.

FROST

Well, one thing, they might got superhuman strength, but you can hurt 'em.

JACOB

Yeah, that bottle upside the head of Santanico didn't kill her, but it didn't feel too good either.

SEX MACHINE

Another thing, you try and ram a broken chair leg in a human, you better be one strong son-of-a-bitch. The human body is one rough-tough machine. But these vamps got soft bodies. The texture of their skin is softer, mushier. You can push shit right through 'em. Conceivably, if you hit one hard enough, you could take their fuckin' head off.

SCOTT

You could take their head off.

SETH

Actually, our best weapon against these satanic
cocksuckers is this man.

(He points at Jacob)

He's a preacher.

Frost and Sex Machine look toward Jacob.

SETH

As far as God's concerned, we might just as well be a
piece of fuckin' shit. But he's one of the boys. Only
one problem, his faith ain't what it used to be.

*Jacob PUNCHES Seth in the mouth, sending him to the floor. Jacob
stands over him.*

JACOB

I've had enough of your taunts.

Seth looks up from the floor.

SETH

I'm not taunting you. We need you. A faithless
preacher doesn't mean shit to us. But a man who's a
servant of God can grab a cross, shove it in these
monsters' asses. A servant of God can bless the tap
water and turn it into a weapon.

Seth rises.

SETH

I know why you lost your faith. How could true

holiness exist if your wife can be taken away from you
and your children? Now, I always said God can kiss
my fuckin' ass. Well, I changed my lifetime tune
about thirty minutes ago 'cause I know, without a
doubt, what's out there trying to get in here is pure
evil straight from hell. And if there is a hell, and those
monsters are from it, there's got to be a heaven. Now
which are you, a faithless preacher or a mean,
motherfuckin' servant of God?

*Jacob has to laugh at that. So does everybody else. Jacob sticks out his
hand and shakes Seth's.*

JACOB
I'm a mean, motherfuckin' servant of God.

*The laughter and good humor passes quickly and the only sound to be
heard is that of the bats gnawing and clawing. It immediately reminds
the group of the deep, deep shit they're in.*

KATE
I don't know if I can take two hours of that noise.

FROST
You can. You'll take it 'cause ya got no choice.
How'd ya like twenty-four hours of it, lying in a
muddy ditch with only the rotting corpses of your
friends to keep you company?

JACOB
What are you talking about?

FROST
Back in '72 I was in Nam, trapped behind enemy

lines, lying in a rat hole with my entire squad dead.
They thought they killed everybody, and except for
me, they were right. But it wasn't for lack of trying. A
grenade blew up right next to me, that's why I'm so
pretty. They thought I was dead, so I played dead.
They dumped all the bodies in a ditch. All I could do
was lie there playing possum. Dead bodies under me,
dead bodies on top of me, listening to the enemy
laugh and joke hour after hour after hour . . .

*As Frost goes into his monologue, the sound fades out and the camera
moves to Sex Machine. He's having a hot flash. He can't hear
anything. He's looking at Frost speaking, but he doesn't hear any
sound. Then he hears a deep, MALE VOICE say:*

> MALE VOICE (V.O.)
>
> Thirst.

*"Who the fuck was that?" he thinks to himself. He turns around:
nobody's there. No one else in the group seems to hear it. A
FEMALE VOICE seductively says:*

> FEMALE VOICE (V.O.)
>
> Thirst.

We hear Sex Machine's thought in a voice answer.

> SEX MACHINE (V.O.)
> Stop fucking saying that!

> TWO MALE VOICES (V.O.)
>
> Thirst!

> SEX MACHINE (V.O.)
> That bite weren't nothin'. It just hurt like a son-of-a-
> bitch, that's all. It barely punched the skin.

Sex Machine looks at Frost, who's acting out his story. The biker is pantomiming fighting and slashing. He's describing all the while, but we can't hear anything. All we hear are many voices, male, female, children saying:

> VOICES (V.O.)
> Thirst . . . Thirst . . . Thirst. . . .

Sex Machine begins looking at the other members of the group in a thirsty way. He stares at each of their necks, closer and closer until he can see the veins on Frost's neck actually pulsating, throbbing, beckoning to him. Sex Machine has turned into a vampire.

The sound comes back as Frost finishes his story.

> FROST
> . . . and then when I came back to my senses, I realized I had killed the entire V.C. squadron singlehandedly. My bayonet had blood and chunks of yellow flesh on it like some cannibal shish kabob. And to this day I don't have the slightest idea how I—

Sex Machine lets out a hideous cry.

> SEX MACHINE
> THIRST!

Frost SCREAMS as Sex Machine grabs hold of him and BITES into his neck.

The group tries to PULL the TWO MEN apart.

Jacob gets his arm around Sex Machine's neck and tries pulling.

Sex Machine takes his teeth out of the biker's neck and SINKS them in Jacob's arm.

Jacob SCREAMS and lets go.

Seth, Kate, and Scott react to Jacob being bit.

Sex Machine GRABS Jacob and TOSSES him effortlessly over the bar, CRASHING into a shelf full of liquor bottles.

Frost HOPS around the room, mad as a hornet, holding his bleeding neck.

FROST
I been bit! He fuckin' bit me!

Sex Machine PUNCHES Seth in the face, dropping him like a sack of potatoes.

He smacks the shit out of Kate. She goes FLYING into a table.

Sex Machine turns, seeing Frost breaking off a big table leg. Frost looks at the big vamp.

FROST

(to Sex Machine)

You're dead, motherfucker! You're gonna bite me!
You just turned me into a vampire, asshole!

SEX MACHINE
What are you gonna do about it?

Frost, table leg in hand, RUNS, SCREAMING his head off, straight at Sex Machine.

Sex Machine's nostrils flare. He raises his meaty fist and pulls it back, so he can really haul off.

Frost, top speed, stake raised, screaming.

Sex Machine lets loose with his punch.

Seth, Scott, and Kate look up from the floor.

Jacob rises from behind the bar.

Frost's face COLLIDES with Sex Machine's fist. Sex Machine hits Frost so hard it lifts the biker off the ground and propels him through the air.

Seth sees where Frost is heading and says:

                    SETH
          Oh shit!

Jacob sees.

                    JACOB
          Good Lord!

Frost, in midair, HITS the barricaded, plastered-over window and CRASHES through it.

Sex Machine lets loose with a maniacal laugh.

Hundreds of bat-things fly into the bar.

Seth grabs the two kids by the hand and runs for the back room.

Behind the bar, Jacob grabs two pieces of wood from off the ground.

Ten bat-things are in hot pursuit of Seth, Kate, and Scott, who are RUNNING for their lives. They get to the door of the back room, whip it open, dive in, and SLAM it behind them. An ugly, fleshy bat-thing manages to get its head caught in the door as it closes. Kate and Scott PUSH on the door as hard as they can. The bat-thing's head, which is inside, screams, howls, and snaps in fury.

Seth turns toward the bat/vamp in the door. He sticks his .45 in its big mouth.

SETH

You wanna suck something, suck on this!

He FIRES four shots that blow the bat vamp's head all over the wall.

Kate yells:

KATE

We have to go back for Daddy!

SETH

Daddy's dead.

KATE

Noooo!

She spins and grabs the door knob, ready to fling the door and help her father. Scott grabs her and pushes her up against the wall.

SCOTT

He's right, Kate. Daddy's dead! It's too damn late, he was too damn far away. If flinging that door and filling this room with those bat-things would save him, I'd fling it. The only thing it'll do is turn us into one of them.

SETH

He needs our help!

SCOTT

He's beyond our help. You saw him get bit. I saw
him get bit. We all saw him get bit. You can't help
him. I've got no one left to lose but you. I can't be
alone again. We're sticking together.

Just then they hear Jacob's voice BOOMING from the barroom.

40 INT. BARROOM—NIGHT

*Jacob, holding a cross made out of two sticks and reciting appropriate
verse from the Bible, is keeping the vampires at bay. But, as Seth
predicted, it is the shining power of his restored faith that is his
mightiest weapon. Jacob is making his way through the vampires,
toward the back door. A lot of the bats have transformed into bat /
devil / human creatures.*

*The creatures stand at the edge of Jacob's force field of holiness. Many
bat-things fly around the bar like mad, whirling dervishes. A cluster of
bat-things over, above, and in front of Jacob. They all growl and hiss
at the man of God. For every one step forward Jacob takes, the
vampires take one step back. Jacob recites the verse from the Bible in a
threatening, mean, motherfucking, servant of God tone. As he speaks
with authority and strength, he sees Frost lying on the ground, bat-
things on him like ants on a candy bar. But Jacob is too much in
control to let even this repugnant sight trip him up.*

Jacob has backed himself up by the door.

JACOB

Open the door!

41

The door FLIES open. Jacob jumps inside. The door SLAMS shut.

Jacob hugs daughter and son. As he hugs them, we see his bloody arm.

When he releases them, they can't help but notice.

SETH

Did he . . . ?

JACOB

Yep.

Seth explodes, knocking over boxes, busting chairs, tipping over tables, and cussing a blue streak.

SETH

Fuck, piss, shit! Motherfuckin' vampires!
Motherfuckin' vampires! *Goddamn motherfuckin'*
vampires!

Seth runs over to the barricaded door and yells to the creatures on the other side.

SETH

You all are gonna fuckin' die! I'm gonna fuckin' kill
every last one of you godless pieces of shit!

JACOB

(to Seth)

> You bet your sweet ass you are, and I'm gonna help
> you do it. But we ain't got much time.

Kate is crying, she knows what's happened to her father.

KATE

You're gonna be okay, aren't you, Daddy?

JACOB

No, I'm not. I've been bit. In effect, I'm already dead.

Scott and Kate, crying, grab their father and hold on for dear life.
Jacob wants to cry, but if he breaks down, the kids will never have the
courage for what they must do.

JACOB

(to his children)

> Children, listen to me. I love you two more than
> anybody. And I just want you to know you've made
> me proud all your lives. But never more so than
> tonight. And I wish we could sit here and cry till I
> pass on, but we can't. Because I'm not going to pass
> on. I'm going to turn into a monster. And when I do,
> I'm going to be dangerous. But before that happens,
> just know I love you.

(to Seth and the kids)

> Now, I'd say in the next twenty or thirty minutes our

friends outside will bust in this door. And I'll probably
turn into a vampire within the hour. Now, you have
two choices. You can wait for me to turn, then deal
with me, then wait for them to burst inside here and
the three of you will deal with them. Or, we can kick
open that door and the four of us can hit 'em with
everything we have, and carve a path right through
'em to the front entrance. But if we're gonna go at
'em, we gotta go at 'em now. I confused them, I
scared them, I took them off guard. But they're going
to get unconfused, they're going to get unscared,
they're going to get together, and they're going to hit
that door like a ton of bricks. And when that moment
arrives, we gotta be ready.

*Jacob sees that the back room is pretty damn big and filled with boxes
and crates.*

JACOB
What's this stuff?

SETH
My guess is that this little dive's been feeding on
nomad road waifs like bikers and truckers for a long
time. This is probably some of the shipments they
stole off the trucks.

JACOB
Well, I say let's tear this place apart for weapons. So
when they burst through that door, we'll make 'em
wish they never did.

SETH
I don't give a shit about living or dying anymore. I

just want to send as many of these devils back to hell
as I can.

                    JACOB

Amen.

42 MONTAGE

*The survivors are opening boxes and prying open crates. A lot of what
they find is bullshit. Pantyhose, coffee, Teddy bears, etc. But a few of
the boxes are just what the doctor ordered. Cases from a sporting good
supplier yield a shipment of baseball bats. Meant to arrive at toy stores
are a shipment of Uzi replica squirt guns and a box of balloons. And
captured en route to a hardware store are shipments of power tools,
saws, and jackhammers.*

Seth and Scott saw the bats into wooden stakes.

*Kate fills the Uzi squirt guns with tap water from the back-room
sink.*

*Jacob, with Seth's knife, etches a cross into every bullet in the .45
automatic's last full clip of ammo.*

A42 VAMPIRES ALL START CONVERGING ON THE
BACK-ROOM DOOR, GETTING THEIR
COURAGE BACK.

Kate makes water balloons.

Scott sharpens the stakes to a point with the tools.

Seth attaches a wooden stake to the end of a jackhammer.

Jacob blesses the water in the squirt guns and balloons, turning it into holy water.

Our heroes work together, preparing for the battle to come. The back-room door, barricaded with crates and boxes, begins to be pounded on by the undead on the other side. The room tone is a combination of chewing, scratching, pounding, squeaking, and screaming.

Finally they're ready.

43 JACOB TURNS TO HIS KIDS.

> JACOB
>
> Before we go any further, I need you three to promise me something. I'll fight with you to the bitter end, but when I turn into one of them, I won't be Jacob anymore. I'll be a lapdog of Satan. I want you three to promise you'll take me down, no different from the rest.

The kids can't say the words.

> SETH
>
> I promise.

> JACOB
>
> Kate, Scott?

KATE
I promise.

                    JACOB
Scott?

                    SCOTT
Yeah, I promise.

Jacob doesn't believe them.

                    JACOB
Why don't I believe you?

(He picks up the .45)

> I'm gonna ask you two again, then I want you to
> swear to God that you'll kill me. If you don't, I'm
> gonna just kill myself right now. Now, since you need
> me, I think you better swear. Kate, do you swear to
> God that when I turn into one of the undead, you'll
> kill me?

Kate doesn't answer. Jacob places the .45 barrel against his temple.

                    JACOB
Kate, we don't have all day, so I'm only gonna count
to five. One . . . two . . . three . . . four . . .

                    KATE
Okay, okay, I promise I'll do it!

                    JACOB
Not good enough, swear to God.

KATE

I swear to God, our Father, that when you change
into one of the undead, I will kill you.

JACOB

Good girl. Now, Scott, we have even less time, so I'm
only giving you the count of three. One . . .

SCOTT

You don't believe in suicide.

JACOB

It's not suicide if you're already dead. Two . . .

SCOTT

Okay, I'll kill you when you change, I swear to God
in Jesus Christ's name.

JACOB

Thank you, son.

SETH

Okay, vampire killers, let's kill some fuckin' vampires.

44 INT. BARROOM—NIGHT

*The vampires, bat-things, and what-have-you start BREAKING
down the door. They are in a mad frenzy. They burst through the
door.*

*Waiting for them are Scott and Kate holding Uzi squirt guns and
water balloons draped down their chests on a belt like grenades. Jacob*

*is holding a cross made of sharp wooden stakes and the .45 with the
cross bullets.*

Seth is holding the jackhammer.

*The survivors walk out of the back room into the bar. The vamps
back up, letting them inside.*

*What we have here is a Mexican standoff, à la "Wild Bunch." A
moment of peace before the battle. The vamps just watch the humans.
The humans just watch the vamps. Then, like the bull in the china
shop, Seth ends the peace by starting up the jackhammer.*

                    SETH
          Kill 'em all!

Jacob holds up the cross, the vamps react.

The kids SPRAY the crowd with UZI fire, burning vampire flesh.

The pack of vamps retreat while the Fuller squad walk forward.

They are attacked on all sides, but they keep moving toward the door.

*Seth slams the stakes into several of the vamps, it speeds in and out of
vampire chests, each time spraying him in green vamp blood.*

*Jacob shoves his cross stake into a vampire with one hand and
SHOOTS three vampires with blessed bullets with the other.*

Flame BURSTS from the vampires' chests when the bullets hit.

*Kate and Scott both whip water balloons off their belts and toss them
into the crowd.*

They burst and FRY several of the vamps, who fall, screaming in pain.

From its perch on a wood ceiling beam, a bat-thing drops and HURLS toward the group.

Jacob sees it, raises his gun, and FIRES.

The bat-thing bursts into a ball of screaming fire.

Seth continues carving a path to the front door by slamming the hammer stake into vampire chests.

The front door is barricaded again by a big table and other junk.

SCOTT

(yelling)

Why did they block the door again?

JACOB

(yelling)

To keep the daylight out! This is where they sleep! Get to the door!

Seth tries to get to the front door, when Sex Machine, now a half-bat, half-devil vamp, about six foot seven, drops from above in front of him. Seth RAMS the stake in its chest. The Sex Machine-thing screams out, LIFTING the hammer and Seth off the ground.

Seth is thrown from his hold on the hammer across the room. He CRASHES into a table.

The Sex Machine-thing falls back with the jackhammer sticking out of his chest, dead.

Kate, spraying Uzi fire like Rambo, sees Seth fall. She screams:

                    KATE
          Seth!

Seth quickly gets up to find himself surrounded by vampires on all sides. With no weapons, he puts up his dukes.

                    SETH
          Okay, deadboys, come on! Take a bite and feel all
          right!

Kate clusters with her father and Scott.

                    KATE

(yelling)

          I'm going for 'em!

                    JACOB
          No!

                    KATE
          Everybody goes home!

Kate turns into a squirtgun-firing, water-balloon-throwing, one-woman army, as she breaks from her father and heads in Seth's direction.

KATE

(screaming)

Die, monster, die! Die, monster, die!

Kate mows down the group by Seth, they lie on the floor, burning in agony. Kate takes Seth's hand and gives him a couple of water balloons and a stake.

KATE

(to Seth)

Watch my back!

SETH

Anytime.

Cutting through vampires, the two make their way across the bar.

Jacob, firing the .45, takes out several more vampires in fiery death.

Scott fires the Uzi and chucks more water balloons.

As Jacob fights, all of a sudden the sound goes out. He can't hear anything. He wonders if he's gone deaf. He starts to hear the words: "Thirst, thirst, thirst." He notices the vampires have stopped attacking him. They look at him with happy smiles on their devilish faces. Fangs begin to grow. His eyes are yellow.

Scott turns to his dad. He sees his father is a monster.

Jacob, with a devilish grin on his face, GRABS Scott and sinks his teeth into Scott's forearm. Scott screams bloody murder as his dad begins to drain him of blood.

Scott takes one of the water balloons he's wearing and SMASHES it against Jacob's head.

The holy water melts half of Jacob's face away. He lets go of Scott, screaming, and drops the .45 on the floor.

Scott drops to the ground, picking up the gun. He brings it up to fire.

A totally evil Jacob, with only half a face, matches stares with the boy he once called his son.

Scott's eyes turn to steel.

SCOTT

I swear to God, in Jesus Christ's name.

He FIRES, sending a holy bullet into Jacob's forehead, creating a hole from which fire shoots out. Jacob's entire head bursts into flames, then explodes.

From across the room, Kate sees her daddy ignite. She cries out. In the thick of the battle, Seth yells:

SETH

Fight now, cry later.

Kate takes his advice and hits a vamp square in the face with a holy water balloon, which melts his head.

A bat-thing lands on the back of Scott's neck. He screams as it bites into him. He drops the .45.

Kate sees Scott get bit.

KATE

Oh my God!

Another bat-thing lands on Scott's arm and takes a bite. Scott screams.

KATE

You bastards!

She goes to spray them when her Uzi runs out of water.

Now seven bat-things are on Scott biting and sucking blood. Scott is in agony.

SCOTT

Kill me Kate!

Kate runs for her brother, does a DIVE and a ROLL, coming up by the .45, SNATCHING it in one motion and FIRING three times.

One . . . two . . . three bat-things are hit, shoot flames, then all of them EXPLODE, BLOWING UP Scott.

The remaining vamps approach.

All the humans have left is a few bullets and one holy balloon.

SETH

How many bullets left, kid?

KATE

Not many.

SETH

Well, when you run out of weapons, just start cold-cocking 'em. Make 'em sing for their supper.

The two survivors are backed up against a wall.

Two bat things do a kamikaze dive from the air toward Seth.

Direct hit. The two bat-things burst into flames and spiral to the floor.

The two survivors look at the vampires, who stand before them. A moment of stillness before the attack. Kate stands holding the .45, arm outstretched.

KATE

(to Seth)

Should I use the last bullets on us?

SETH
You use 'em on the first couple of these parasites that try to bite you.

The vamps begin to close in. Kate lines up the .45 sights on the face of an approaching vampire.

Seth holds the Uzi like a club, ready to bash in the first vampire's head that gets in swinging distance.

Beams of sunlight shoot through the holes that Kate shot through the wall. Approaching vampires burn. The scorched vamps scream like they've never screamed before.

SETH
Shoot more holes!

Kate turns away from the vamps and shoots holes in the wall behind him. Daylight comes through, providing Kate and Seth with a safe, lighted area.

The .45's empty.

The vamps hiss and scream at the frustration of not being able to get at them.

The two survivors hold hands, when . . .

All of a sudden the door to the Titty Twister is pounded on from the outside.

The vamps look toward it in horror.

From the other side of the door, we hear a voice with a Spanish accent.

VOICE (O.S.)

(in Spanish)

> I'm looking for my friend. Is Seth in there?

Seth's face lights up like Rome burning.

SETH

(yelling)

> Carlos!

(in Spanish)

> Help us, bash the door in. Bash the door in!

CARLOS (O.S.)

(in Spanish)

> Danny, Manny, knock down the door. Hurry, hurry!

The vamps are totally fucking freaked out! They run and fly around the bar in a panic. Crying, howling, grabbing onto each other.

The front door is TORN apart from shotgun fire coming from the outside, punching holes the size of basketballs in the door.

The table in front of the door gives and FALLS forward.

The door caves in and sunlight invades the bar. Many vamps are instantly fried, bursting into flames.

The Mexican gangster CARLOS and his two henchmen, DANNY and MANNY, are horrified at what they see. They cross themselves in fright.

Vampires search for dark corners, but all is lost. Sunlight hits a mirrored ball attached to the ceiling, sending hundred of beams of sunlight scattering through the room. Vamps try and dodge the beams. No dice. All around the bar vamps combust in fiery explosions.

The Titty Twister is now on fire, burning out of control.

Seth and Kate run through the burning building and leap through the door into the parking lot.

45 EXT. TITTY TWISTER PARKING LOT— MORNING

Carlos, Danny, and Manny help them to their feet and walk them away from the blazing bar. They catch their breath by Carlos's Mercedes.

CARLOS

(to Seth)

What the fuck was going on in there?

*Seth signals Carlos to wait a minute while he catches his breath.
Then he hauls off and PUNCHES Carlos square in the kisser.
Danny and Manny aim their shotguns at Seth.*

CARLOS

(in Spanish)

Whatsamatter with you? Are you crazy?

SETH

Why the fuck, outta all the godforsaken shitholes in
Mexico, did you have us rendezvous at that place?

CARLOS

I don't know, one place's as good as another.

SETH

Have you ever been there before?

CARLOS

No, but I passed by it a couple of times. It's out in the
middle of nowhere. It seems like a rowdy place, so
there wouldn't be a lot of police. And it's open from
dusk till dawn. You said meet you in the morning.

SETH

Well, because you picked that place out of a hat, my
brother's dead now. And this girl's family's dead.

Carlos stands up again.

CARLOS

I'm sorry to hear that. What were they, psychos?

SETH

Did they look like psychos? They were fuckin'
vampires. Psychos don't explode when sunlight hits
'em, I don't care how crazy they are.

*Danny and Manny react to the vampire news by crossing themselves
again.*

CARLOS

Oh, Seth, how can I ever make it up to you?

SETH

You can't, but fifteen percent instead of thirty for my
stay at El Ray is a good start.

CARLOS

Twenty-eight.

SETH

Jesus Christ, Carlos, my brother's dead and he's not
coming back, and it's all your fault. Twenty.

They look at each other, then shake hands, saying in unison:

SETH AND CARLOS

Twenty-five.

(pause)

Deal!

TIME CUT:

Trunk of Seth's new Porsche is opened. The suitcase full of money is placed inside.

CARLOS

Do you like the car?

SETH

It looks great, but I said like new. This is a "90."

CARLOS

But it is like new. It belonged to a friend of mine—drug dealer—only drove it fourteen times in five years. Swear to God. That's like new.

SETH

So do I just follow you?

CARLOS

Yeah, follow us.

SETH

Let's do it.

CARLOS

(to Danny and Manny)

Vamanos!

Carlos, Danny, and Manny pile into Carlos's white Mercedes.

Seth, by his Porsche, looks back at Kate.

Kate stands alone.

The whole desert seems between them.

So much to say . . . but no words.

> SETH
>
> I'm sorry.

> KATE
>
> Me too.

Long pause.

> SETH
>
> See ya.

> KATE
>
> Later.

Seth turns his back on her. Just as he opens the door, Kate says behind him:

> KATE (O.S.)
>
> Seth.

Seth turns around.

> KATE
>
> You want some company?

Seth smiles.

> SETH
>
> Kate honey, I may be a bastard. But I'm not a fuckin' bastard.

He blows her a kiss across the desert.

She blows one back.

Seth's in his car and GONE.

Kate turns around, faces the endless desert before her, and begins her long walk home.

THEME OF MOVIE BEGINS POUNDING

The End

credits and cast list

MIRAMAX

Miramax Films Presents

A BAND APART

In Association With
LOS HOOLIGANS PRODUCTIONS

A ROBERT RODRIGUEZ FILM

from dusk till dawn

HARVEY KEITEL
GEORGE CLOONEY
QUENTIN TARANTINO
and JULIETTE LEWIS

SALMA HAYEK
BRENDA HILLHOUSE
MARC LAWRENCE
CHEECH MARIN
MICHAEL PARKS
KELLY PRESTON

TOM SAVINI
JOHN SAXON
DANNY TREJO
FRED WILLIAMSON

and introducing
ERNEST LIU
as Scott Fuller

Casting By
JOHANNA RAY, C.S.A.
& ELAINE J. HUZZAR

Special Makeup Effects By
KURTZMAN, NICOTERO & BERGER EFX GROUP, INC.

Music By
GRAEME REVELL

Costume Designer
GRACIELA MAZÓN

Production Designer
CECILIA MONTIEL

Editor
ROBERT RODRIGUEZ

Director of Photography
GUILLERMO NAVARRO

Co-Producers
ELIZABETH AVELLÁN
PAUL HELLERMAN
ROBERT KURTZMAN
JOHN ESPOSITO

Executive Producers
LAWRENCE BENDER

ROBERT RODRIGUEZ
QUENTIN TARANTINO

Story By
ROBERT KURTZMAN

Screenplay By
QUENTIN TARANTINO

Produced By
GIANNI NUNNARI
MEIR TEPER

Directed By
ROBERT RODRIGUEZ

In Order of Appearance

Texas Ranger Earl McGraw	MICHAEL PARKS
Pete Bottoms	JOHN HAWKES
Seth Gecko	GEORGE CLOONEY
Red-Headed Hostage	HEIDI MCNEAL
Richard Gecko	QUENTIN TARANTINO
Blonde Hostage	AIMEE GRAHAM
Jacob Fuller	HARVEY KEITEL
Kate Fuller	JULIETTE LEWIS
Scott Fuller	ERNEST LIU
Old Timer	MARC LAWRENCE
Hostage Gloria	BRENDA HILLHOUSE
Newscaster Kelly Houge	KELLY PRESTON
FBI Agent Stanley Chase	JOHN SAXON
Border Guard	CHEECH MARIN
Chet Pussy	CHEECH MARIN
Titty Twister Guitarist & Vocalist	TITO LARRIVA
Titty Twister Saxophonist	PETE ATASANOFF
Titty Twister Drummer	JOHNNY VATOS HERNANDEZ
Razor Charlie	DANNY TREJO
Big Emilio	ERNEST GARCIA
Danny the Wonder Pony	DANNY THE WONDER PONY

Sex Machine	TOM SAVINI
Frost	FRED WILLIAMSON
Santanico Pandemonium	SALMA HAYEK
Mouth Bitch Victim	GINO CROGNALE
Santanico Victim	GREG NICOTERO
Carlos	CHEECH MARIN
Danny	CRISTOS
Manny	MIKE MOROFF
Bar Dancers	MICHELLE BERUBE
	NEENA BIDASHA
	VEENA BIDASHA
	UNGELA BROCKMAN
	MADISON CLARK
	MARIA DIAZ
	ROSALIA HAYAKAWA
	JANINE JORDAE
	JACQUE LAWSON
	HOUSTON LEIGH
	JANIE LISZEWSKI
	TIA TEXADA
Stunt Coordinator	STEVE DAVISON
Stunt Players	WILLIAM ATWELL
	ROBIN BONACCORSI
	ROBERT F. BROWN
	TROY T. BROWN
	MICHELE BURKETT
	WILLIAM H. BURTON
	JENNIFER J. CAPUTO
	SAMUEL D'AURIA
	STEVE DAVISON
	TIM DAVISON
	FREDDIE HICE
	RICARDO GAONA
	LANCE GILBERT
	TROY GILBERT
	NADINE GRYCAN

RANDALL J. HALL
TOM HARPER
ANITA HARTSHORN
ACE HATEM
DANA HEE
STEVE HOLLADAY
BILLY H. HOOKER
BUDDYJOE HOOKER
THOMAS HUFF
JEFFREY IMADA
MATT JOHNSTON
HENRY KINGI
BILLY (WILLIAM) LUCAS
GARY McLARTY
BENNIE MOORE JR.
GREG NICOTERO
HUGH AODH O'BRIEN
MARINA A. OVIEDO
MANNY PERRY
CHAD RANDALL
TROY ROBINSON
DANNY ROGERS
ERIK L. RONDELL
FRANK TORRES
TIMOTHY P. TRELLA
SCOTT WILDER
SPICE WILLIAMS

Monsters   JON FIDELE
MICHAEL MCKAY
JAKE McKINNON
JOSH PATTON
WALTER PHELAN
WAYNE TOTH
HENRIK VON RYZIN

Production Manager   PAUL HELLERMAN

Post Production Supervisor   TAMARA SMITH

Visual Effects Supervisors	DAN FORT
	ELIZABETH AVELLAN
	DIANA DRU BOTSFORD
1st Assistant Director	DOUGLAS AARNIOKOSKI
2nd Assistant Director	BRIAN BETTWY
2nd 2nd Assistant Director	DIETER "DIETMAN" BUSCH
Production Accountant	STEVE BEESON
Assistant Accountant	CHERYL "VENUS" VENTURA
Accounting Assistant	DANIEL MYERS BOONE
Production Coordinator	DAWN TODD
Asst. Production Coordinator	CATHY AGCAYAB
Production Secretary	JEFF SWAFFORD
Key Office Production Assistants	LAURA "CAPTAIN" RUSH
	JOHN PATRICK HARDIN
Script Supervisor	LOU ANN QUAST
Location Manager	ROBERT E. CRAFT
Location Assistants	KYLE OLIVER
	DOUGLAS DRESSER
Camera Operator	ROBERT RODRIGUEZ
Camera Operator	GUILLERMO NAVARRO
1st Assistant Camera	ZIAD DOUEIRI
1st Assistant Camera	ALAN COHEN
2nd Assistant Camera	TIMOTHY KANE
2nd Assistant Camera	CAMILLE R. FREER
Steadicam Operator	ROBERT RODRIGUEZ
Add'l Steadicam Operator	DAVID CHAMEIDES
Film Loader	DAVID E. BERRYMAN
Camera Intern	PATRICK TACKETT
Production Sound Mixer	MARK ULANO
Boom Operators	PATRUSHKHA MIERZWA
	GLORIA COOPER
Sound Intern	CHRIS SPOSA
Key Hair/Make-Up Artist	ERMAHN OSPINA

Assistant Hair/Make-Up	DON MALOT
Assistants Make-Up	HEIDI GROTSKY
	DEBORAH NOELLE THURIN
Tattoo Artist	GILL MONTIE
Costume Supervisor	JACQUELINE ARONSON
Assistant to Costume Designer	BRITT THORPE SHERWOOD
Set Costumer	JILLIAN KREINER
Costumer	C. HOUSTON SAMS
Set Costumer Assistant	IRERI MAZON
Wardrobe Intern	NATHAN EASTERLING
Gaffer	DAVID LEE
Best Boy Electric	ANDREW T. WATTS
	NATHAN HATHAWAY
Electricians	HEATHER HILLMEYER
	FLINT ELLSWORTH
	LENNON BASS, JR.
Key Grip	RICK STRIBLING
Best Boy Grip	JAMES B. "CRASH" IRONS
	TIM "STUFFY" SORONEN
Dolly Grip	BOB IVANJACK
Grips	JASON "JAKE" CROSS
	VANCE COHEN
	JEREMY LAUNAIS
Grip Intern	BRYAN SWERLING
Art Director	MAYNE SCHUYLER BERKE
Set Decorator	FELIPE FERNANDEZ del PASO
Lead Man	CHRIS CARRIVEAU
Set Designer	COLIN de ROUIN
Property Masters	STEVE JOYNER
	CAYLAH EDDLEBLUTHE
Assistant Property Master	MARTIN MILLIGAN
Special Weapons Designer	STEVE JOYNER

On-Set Dresser	McPHERSON O'REILLY DOWNS
Buyer	JENNIE HARRIS
Art Department Coordinator	ABIGAIL SHEINER
Set Dressers	KEN CARRIVEAU
	GREGG M. HARTMAN
	MICHAEL WHETSTONE
	JEFF HAY
	PAUL DOWLER
	HOWARD P. MILLER
Swing Gang	STEVEN INGRASSIA
	MICHAEL J. BRADY
	RONALD RUSSOM
	CHRISTINE GEBELE
Assistant Art Director	ADAM LUSTIG
Assistant Set Decorator	MARY PATVALDNIEKS
Art Dept. Production Assistant	MELISSA L. HALE
Art Dept. Interns	BETO CASILLAS
	AMY MONTGOMERY
	JENNIFER MARTINEZ
	ADAM NAGEL
Construction Coordinator	BRIAN MARKEY
Construction Foreman	MICHAEL ATWELL
Lead Carpenter	SHANE HAWKINS
Construction Estimator	CHRIS SCHER
Lead Scenic	MARCO GILLSON
Scenic Carpenters	CHRIS BARNES
	COLIN BARDON
	JAMES M. DRURY
	BRUCE HARRIS
	SHAWN HAWKINS
	MARK PETERS
	RAMSEY SMITH
	JAMES STANBERRY
	FLOYD R. VALERO
On-Set Carpenter	SCOT CUMMINGS

Painters	JAMES C. BEESON
	JENNIFER FLYNN
	WENDY JERDE
	ADAM MARKEY
	PEDRO V. SUCHITE
	CARLOS A. CHAVEZ
Laborer	OSWALDO ROJAS
Sculptors	ALEX BOGARTZ
	BOB CLARK
	LARRY E. McCAULEY
	DAVID SHWARTZ
Titty Twister Sign By	GERALD MARTINEZ
1st Assistant Editor	DANIEL A. FORT
Assistant Editors	ETHAN MANIQUIS
	JOAQUIN G. AVELLAN
Music Editor	JOSHUA WINGET
Music Consultants	MARY RAMOS
	CHUCK KELLEY
Dialogue Coach for Mr. Keitel	JON SPERRY
Unit Publicist	KATHERINE MOORE &
	ASSOCIATES
Unit Still Photographer	JOYCE RUDOLPH
Casting Assistant	MARY JANE LAVACCA
Extras Casting By	RAINBOW CASTING
Assistant to Mr. Bender	COURTNEY McDONNELL
Assistant to Mr. Rodriguez	MARK THORNHILL
Assistant to Mr. Tarantino	VICTORIA LUCAI
Assistant to Mr. Clooney	AMY MINDA COHEN
Assistant to Mr. Keitel	LOREN LOCKWOOD
Assistant to Co-Producers	CORINNE T. NEEDLE
Key Set Production Assistant	BEN PARKER
Set Production Assistants	JAY Y. BEATTIE
	TERESA DELUCIO
	AARON PENN

Office Production Interns	GEOFF HALE
	LOWELL NORTHROP
	PERI SILVERMAN
Make-Up FX Supervisors	ROBERT KURTZMAN
	GREG NICOTERO
	HOWARD BERGER
Make-Up FX Designer/Illustrator	JOHN BISSON
Make-Up FX Coordinator	KAMAR BITAR
Make-Up FX Shop Foreman	SHANNON SHEA
Make-Up FX Key Personnel	GINO CROGNALE
	WAYNE TOTH
	NORMAN CABRERA
	CHRISTOPHER ROBBINS
	HENRIK VAN RYZIN
Sculptors	MARK ALFREY
	EVAN CAMPBELL
	MARK TAVARES
	GREG SMITH
Moldmakers	MIKE McCARTY
	ERIC HARRIS
	ALAN TUSKES
Mechanics	JEFF EDWARDS
	JAKE McKINNON
	LUKE KHANLIAN
	HIROSHI IKEUCHI
	MARIO CASTILLO
	LARRY ODIEN
	DAVID KINDLON
Lab Technicians	BRIAN RAE
	JOHN FIDELE
	TED HAINEE
	DAVID WOGH
	NICK MARRA
	GARY JONES
	ROB HINDERSTEIN
	WILLIAM HUNT
	RODD MATSUI

	MATTHEW TRAVISON
	MICHAEL DUDLEY
Hair Technicians	ROBERT MAVERICK
	JILLIAN GLASS
	MELANIE TOOKER
	DOUG NOE
	AUDREY GOETZ
	CONSTANCE GRAYSON
	RON PIPES
Seamstresses	MARY KAY JENSEN
	LOVELYNN VANDERHORST
	STEPHANIE WISE
Runners	KARRIE AUBUCHON
	JEREMY PADOW
Mechanical/Pyro FX	BELLISSIMO/BELARDINELLI EFFECTS, INC.
Mechanical FX Coordinator	T. "BROOKLYN" BELLISSIMO
Mechanical FX Key	CHARLES "O.G." BELARDI-NELLI
Mechanical FX Assistants	SHANNON "GATO" THOMPSON
	CHRISTY "THE GIRL" SUMNER
	JOHNNY FRANCO III
	FRANKIE IUDICA JR.
	THOMAS "T2" LIBERTO
	CARY STUART
	MALIA KAUILANI THOMPSON
Mechanical FX P.A.	JACK M. HARVEY
Transportation Coordinator	DEREK "SPEED" RASER
Transportation Captains	"COUSIN" BOB McCORD
	J.T. "THE FINGER" THAYER II
Drivers	BRUCE "KIRBY" CALLAHAN
	JEFF "KAHUNA" COFFMAN
	PAUL "ROSEBUD" BURLIN
	STEVE "EASY MONEY" EARLE
	DON "GONE" FEENEY

SCOTT "GOODY"
GOUDREAU
JASON "JUNIOR" McCORD
MACK "THE KNIFE"
McINVILLE
"LONESOME" GEORGE
NADIAN
TOM "THE SWITCH"
O'DONNELL
GEOFF "T-BONE"
TEAGARDIN
EARL "MR. BLONDE"
THIELEN
TRACY "ACE" THIELEN

Stand-Ins WILLIAM ATWELL
PAM ROSENBERG

Medic/Stage Manager TAYLOR A. CUMMINGS
Studio Teacher JAN D. TYS
Set Security By TECHNICAL GUARD
SECURITY, NICK ROBERTS,
SUPERVISOR
Production Catering By MARIO'S CATERING
Craft Service KEN BONDY
Craft Service Assistant ANDREW T. ROTHMUND

A Band Apart Legal CARLOS GOODMAN, LICHTER,
GROSSMAN & NICHOLS, INC.
Los Hooligans Legal CRAIG EMANUEL, SINCLAIR,
TENENBAUM & OLESIUK
Music Legal Services MYMAN, ABELL, FINEMAN,
GREENSPAN & ROWAN

Labor Attorney RICHARD W. KOPENHEFER
Insurance Providers GREAT NORTHERN/REIFF &
ASSOCIATES
Completion Guarantors FILM FINANCES, INC., KURT
WOOLNER & MAUREEN
DUFFY

Snakes Provided By	REPTILE RENTALS
Trainer	JULES SYLVESTER
Dogs Provided By	COUGAR HILL RANCH
Trainers	NICHOLAS TOTH
	CHANDRA MARRS
	ALVIN MEARS
Video Playback Provided By	PLAYBACK TECHNOLOGIES

Visual Effects Photography

Visual Effects Director	DIANA DRU BOTSFORD
Script Supervisor	ROCHELLE GROSS
1st Assistant Director	DAVID VINCENT RIMER
Director of Photography	JAMES BELKIN
Assistant Camera	RUDY PAHOYO
	GARY ANDERTON

Gaffer	ERIC S. FOSTER
Additional Gaffer	BRIAN T. LOUKS
Key Grip	JOHN WARNER
Additional Key Grip	KEVIN WADOWSKI
Griptrician	JOSE RICARDO "STICK SHIFT" MARTINEZ
	TAYLOR SPARKS
	JASON ELIAS
Video Effects Switcher Operator	JEFF BURRAGE
Production Assistants	JACK M. HARVEY
	NICOLE HEARON
	TODD LINCOLN

Additional Photography—Mexico Unit

Unit Production Manager	LUZ MARIA ROJAS
First Assistant Camera	GERARDO MANJARREZ
Production Assistants	TOMMY NIX
	DAN SHAW

| Visual Effects Coordinator | ROCHELLE GROSS |
| Pre-Visualization Artist | GINA WARR |

Digital Imagery/Compositing By The Post Group

Executive Producer of Visual FX	MARK FRANCO
Creative Director/	
Sr. Digital Compositor	PETER STERNLICHT
Digital Compositor	STEVE SCOTT
Visual FX Producer	KAREN SKOURAS
Digital Film Scanning & Recording	CHRISTOPHER KUTCKA
Digital Data Coordinator	LINDA CORDELLA
Digital Systems Engineer	JOE DAVENPORT
Visual FX Animator	GENEVIEVE YEE
Visual FX Animator	JULIE GLAZER
Visual FX Trainee	AHRYN SCOTT

CGI Bat Visual Effects By VIFX

Rhonda C. Gunner, Richard E. Hollander, Gregory L. McMurry, John C. Wash

Visual FX Supervisor	JOHN C. WASH
Visual FX Producer	JOSH R. JAGGARS
Digital Supervisor	JOHN (D.J.) DESJARDIN
3D CGI Supervisor	ANTOINE DURR
Animator	MORRIS MAY
Simulation Software	ANDY KOPRA
Digital Compositing Supervisor	CHERYL BUDGETT
2nd Team	TONY DIEP
	HARRY LAM
	EDWIN RIVERA
	GREGORY ELLWOOD
Art Director/Matte Artist	KAREN DEJONG

Custom 3D Bat Datasets Provided By Viewpoint Datalabs International

Matte Painting By Illusion Arts, Inc.

Visual Effects Supervisor	ROBERT STROMBERG
Production Manager	CATHERINE SUDOLCAN
Matte Photography	MARK SAWICKI
Digital Matte Artist	MIKE WASSEL
Matte Effects	LYNN LEDGERWOOD

Post Production Accountant	CHERYL "VENUS" VENTURA
Post Production Assistants	LAURA "CAPTAIN" RUSH
Supervising Sound Editor	DEAN BEVILLE
Sound Editors	GREGORY HEDGEPATH
	CHARLES EWING SMITH
	CHARLES MAYNES
	PATRICIO LIEBENSON
	ALLAN BROMBERG
Dialogue Editor	FRANK SMATHERS
Supervising ADR Editor	HARRY MILLER III
ADR Editor	BETH BERGERON
Foley Editors	SCOTT CURTIS
	SOLANGE BOISSEAU
Foley Walkers	SEAN ROWE
	LAURA MACIAS
Sound Recordist	MATT BEVILLE
Assistant Sound Editor	DANA GUSTAFSON
Apprentice Sound Editor	THOMAS FABRICANTE
	BOB WISHNEFSKY
ADR/Foley Recordist	DANA PORTER
ADR/Foley Mixer	ROBERT DESCHAINE, C.A.S.
Re-Recording Facilities	TWENTIETH CENTURY FOX
	SOUND DEPARTMENT
Re-Recording Mixers	SERGIO REYES
	TENNYSON SEBASTIAN II
	ROBERT RODRIGUEZ
	THOMAS P. GERARD
Dubbing Recordist	TIM GOMILLION
Loader	CARRIE MINKLER
Stage Engineer	GARY W. CARLSON
Dubbing Projectionist	JOHN BATES
Color Timer	DAVID ORR
Negative Cutter	MO HENRY

Dolby Stereo Consultant   THOM "COACH" EHLE

**Original Motion Picture Soundtrack Available on Epic CDs and
Cassettes**

Special Thanks To:

ADIDAS
ROBERT BLAKE
HUGO BOSS
(ANHEUSER–BUSCH) BUDWEISER
CATERPILLAR, INC.
CINEMA ONE SPECTRUM
CONVERSE
FAT DOG AND RAIDER
JOEL FITZPATRICK
BRIAN GERSH
GEORGE GOMEZ
CRAIG HAMMON
HARLEY DAVIDSON
ICEE
KEDS
SHELDON LETTICH
MOSSIMO WOMEN
ROBERT NEWMAN
NIKE
CLAUDIA ORTIZ
PCL
PLACE IT ENTERTAINMENT
SALVADOR QUIROZ
TERESA RODRIGUEZ
RONA
SALVATION NAVY
DIEGO SANDOVAL
MIKE SIMPSON
SNACK KING
JIM THOMPSON
TURTLE BEACH
UPP

JOHN WELLS
JIM WILSON

Special Thanks to the Cities of Barstow and Lancaster
and Scott Spiegel

STOCK FOOTAGE PROVIDED BY
FILM & VIDEO STOCK SHOTS

GRIP AND ELECTRIC EQUIPMENT PROVIDED BY
HOLLYWOOD RENTALS

CAMERAS PROVIDED BY
OTTO NEMENZ

CAMERA DOLLY PROVIDED BY
J. L. FISHER, INC.

TITLES & OPTICALS BY
CINEMA RESEARCH CORPORATION

ORIGINATED ON EASTMAN COLOR NEGATIVE

COLOR BY
TECHNICOLOR

SDDS   DOLBY ® SR
                                          IN SELECTED THEATERS

THE ANIMALS USED IN THIS FILM WERE IN NO WAY MIS-TREATED AND ALL SCENES IN WHICH THEY APPEARED WERE FILMED UNDER STRICT SUPERVISION WITH THE UTMOST CONCERN FOR THEIR HANDLING.

THIS MOTION PICTURE IS PROTECTED UNDER LAWS OF THE UNITED STATES AND OTHER COUNTRIES. ANY UNAUTHORI-ZED EXHIBITION, DISTRIBUTION, OR REPRODUCTION OF THIS MOTION PICTURE OR VIDEO TAPE OR ANY PART THEREOF (INCLUDING THE SOUNDTRACK) MAY RESULT IN SEVERE CIVIL AND CRIMINAL PENALTIES.